"I love you, too," Todd whispered, bending over to press a tiny, gentle kiss on each of Elizabeth's cheeks. "Now, promise me you won't worry about a thing. Go straight upstairs, hop into bed, and have sweet dreams till I see you again in the morning."

Elizabeth laughed. "I promise," she said softly.

She opened the door and stepped into the foyer. Immediately she heard angry voices coming from the den.

"I'm sick and tired of this, Alice. We haven't had dinner together as a family in ages. You're never home, and when you are home, you're working! What kind of life is this?"

Her father sounded furious. And Mrs. Wakefield's retorts were just as sharp, just as angry.

Elizabeth felt all the joy from her evening with Todd rush out of her. Her eyes filled with tears. It was a rude shock, coming home from a wonderful time . . . to this.

She didn't even bother telling her parents she was home. She just ran straight upstairs to her bedroom. Closing the door behind her, she burst into tears.

Bantam Books in the Sweet Valley High Series
Ask your bookseller for the books you have missed

SWEET VALLEY HIGH

TROUBLE AT HOME

Written by
Kate William

Created by
FRANCINE PASCAL

BANTAM BOOKS
NEW YORK · TORONTO · LONDON · SYDNEY · AUCKLAND

RL 6, IL age 12 and up

TROUBLE AT HOME
A Bantam Book / May 1990

Sweet Valley High is a registered trademark of Francine Pascal

Conceived by Francine Pascal

Produced by Daniel Weiss Associates, Inc.
33 West 17th Street
New York, NY 10011

Cover art by James Mathewuse

ISBN 0-553-28518-1

Published simultaneously in the United States and Canada

PRINTED IN THE UNITED STATES OF AMERICA

O   0 9 8 7 6 5 4 3 2 1

TROUBLE AT HOME

One

Elizabeth Wakefield swung open the front door of the split-level house and slipped her key back into her bookbag. "Hello," she called into the foyer. "Anybody home?"

Silence greeted her. "Hey, Prince," she called, but not even the Wakefields' golden retriever greeted her. She could hear a breeze rustling the trees outside, but otherwise everything was quiet. Elizabeth frowned and headed into the kitchen. It wasn't unusual to find the house empty at five o'clock, especially on a Monday, when Jessica, Elizabeth's twin sister, had cheerleading practice. Both of the twins' parents worked—their father at a law firm, their mother as a partner in an interior design company. But somehow the house felt different lately when Elizabeth got home. Emptier, she thought, as she wandered into the kitchen.

The red light on the answering machine was

1

blinking, and Elizabeth pushed the rewind button, then helped herself to a glass of juice as she listened to the messages. There were four. She giggled. The first three were from boys calling for Jessica. That wasn't a surprise. Jessica was one of the most popular girls at Sweet Valley High, and certainly one of the most fickle! The fourth message was from her mother, who sounded distressed. "Hi, everyone, it's Mom. It's four o'clock, and I'm just about to go into a meeting. Looks like I won't be able to come home before the fund-raiser tonight. Could you come and pick me up at the office? We can head off straight from here. Thanks. Can't wait to see you."

Elizabeth leaned back against the counter and took a small sip of juice. Her face brightened as she listened to her mother's message. She was looking forward to the fund-raising party that evening. The dinner and reception were to be held in the garden of a civic center in downtown Sweet Valley. All five Wakefields—the twins, their parents, and Steven, the twins' older brother, a freshman at a nearby state university—were backing Peter Santelli for mayor of the community. Mr. Santelli, Sweet Valley's planning commissioner, was well-liked and respected, and tonight's dinner was one of the first major fund-raisers of his campaign. Elizabeth was looking forward not only to the party itself, but also to the prospect of spending an evening with her whole family. Lately both of her parents were so busy, it seemed as though she hardly saw them. Her father had been especially distant in the past few weeks.

Elizabeth replayed the messages and wrote down the ones that were for Jessica. She was just about to go upstairs when the back door flew open and Jessica burst in, her blond hair flying. Prince Albert was jumping up and down in excited circles, wrapping his leash around Jessica's ankles. "I got home before you did," Jessica chided her twin, "and poor Prince hadn't been out for ages! He was so happy to see me, he practically knocked me over."

Elizabeth gave her twin a wry smile. Trust Jessica to take the one household chore she'd done all month and make it seem like the labors of Hercules! "Jess, you got a bunch of messages," she told her sister, passing her a slip of paper that contained the names and numbers.

"Thanks. I saw that there were messages, but I didn't have time to listen because I had to walk Prince *first*," Jessica said, giving her sister a stern look.

"Right, Jess. You're such a responsible person."

Jessica ignored her twin as she studied the messages. "Mmm," she murmured. "Ben . . .

David . . . I wonder what he wants." She folded up the paper and slipped it into the pocket of her jeans.

"And Mom called. She's running late, so we're supposed to pick her up at work on our way to the fund-raiser tonight," Elizabeth said.

Jessica's blue-green eyes were shining. "Do you think Mr. Santelli will win, Liz?" she asked. "Wouldn't it be exciting if the father of one of my fellow cheerleaders became mayor of Sweet Valley?" Maria Santelli, Mr. Santelli's daughter, attended Sweet Valley High with the twins. "Maybe once Maria is the mayor's daughter she'll invite me to all sorts of great political parties. The entire cheerleading squad will probably go to Washington to meet the President."

Elizabeth laughed. "Running for mayor is a big job, Jess, but I don't think Mr. Santelli will be going to the White House. And I know you won't be." She gave her sister a playful jab in the ribs. "I didn't think you and Maria were all that close, anyway."

Jessica opened the refrigerator and took out a diet soda. "Honestly, Liz. You think you know everything about me just because we're twins. Maria and I happen to be extremely close. I spend at least three days a week after school with her, remember? And we do all kinds of stuff together."

4

"Right, during cheerleading practice," Elizabeth commented. "Although I did notice you and Lila eating lunch with Maria the other day. I don't suppose that has anything to do with the fact that her father is running for mayor now, does it?" Maria had always been friendlier with Elizabeth than with Jessica, until recently, when Jessica had taken a sudden interest in her.

"For your information," Jessica said coldly, "Maria considers me a true friend." She pushed a lock of golden hair behind her ear. "Anyway, I'm going to get ready. I don't have time to stand around here and argue."

Elizabeth was tempted to laugh, but she knew her twin well enough to sense this would turn Jessica's pout into real anger. However often, and however dramatically, she and Jessica disagreed, they knew each other inside out. They were extraordinarily close and would do anything in the world to help each other. Being that close, and looking exactly alike, was what made the twinship so special.

Elizabeth bent down to pet Prince Albert. "Jess and I may look alike, but we sure don't act alike. Right, Prince?" she murmured. The dog gave a yelp that Elizabeth was sure meant he agreed. It was true. As far as looks went, she and Jessica were carbon copies, or clones, as Steven liked to call them. Both girls had long, silky blond hair, blue-green eyes, clear peaches-and-cream complexions, and perfect size-six figures. But as Elizabeth's boyfriend, Todd Wilkins, often remarked, their behavior was as different as night was from day.

Jessica was four minutes younger than her twin sister, and those four minutes seemed to have made all the difference! While Elizabeth liked to read, spend time with Todd or a few close friends, or write articles and a column for Sweet Valley High's newspaper, *The Oracle*, Jessica loved fun, excitement, and change. All the extracurricular activities she chose at school were high visibility, like cheerleading or membership in Pi Beta Alpha, an exclusive school sorority. With such different temperaments, it was only natural that the twins disagreed as often as they did. It was part of what made life around the Wakefield house so interesting.

Elizabeth's reverie was broken by the sound of the telephone. She grabbed it before it rang a second time. "Hello?"

"Jessica?"

"Nope, Liz," she said.

"Whoops, wrong clone. Guess where I am?" her brother asked her.

Elizabeth laughed. "I don't know, Steve. Mars?"

6

"I'm at the bus station. I'll be home in twenty minutes. I just didn't want you to leave without me for the fund-raiser." Steven had recently broken his arm in a hang-gliding accident, so he wasn't able to drive his car.

Elizabeth laughed. "No chance of that. It looks like we're all running a little later than we'd thought, though. Otherwise, I'd pick you up."

"Oh, that's OK," Steven said cheerfully. "I'll grab a taxi. See you soon!"

Elizabeth felt her spirits lifting as she hung up the phone. She was really excited about the evening ahead. It had been a long, long time since the entire family had done something like this together. *Which just means tonight will be all the more special*, Elizabeth told herself.

Elizabeth, Jessica, Steven, and their father were in high spirits as they drove downtown and parked at the side entrance of the building where Alice Wakefield's interior design company had its offices. There was no sign of Mrs. Wakefield yet, and the four of them continued talking and joking as they waited for her. Elizabeth felt secretly relieved to see her father in such a good mood for a change. Lately he hadn't seemed himself. He'd been unusually sensitive about his work. He would complain about his

7

career as a lawyer; yet be resistant to advice or discussion about it. He claimed that serving the law just wasn't the profession it once was. For some reason, he no longer felt that it was worthwhile, and he'd been urging the twins and Steven to make sure they found more gratifying work than he had. His bad mood had affected all of them and the twins and Steven had noticed that he and their mother had been arguing a lot. Since Mr. Santelli's decision to run for mayor, however, Mr. Wakefield had been acting much more like his old self. He'd really thrown himself into the campaign, and much of his old energy and lightheartedness had come back.

"Tonight should be wonderful. Steve, I'm surprised you were able to make it from school. Glad, but surprised," Mr. Wakefield commented. He glanced out the window, looking for Mrs. Wakefield. "Sometimes I forget what it's like to be a carefree college student," he added. He said it teasingly, but there was a wistful note in his voice. Elizabeth wondered if this was one of those times when he was feeling less than a hundred percent thrilled with his job.

"Yeah, well, you know what it's like, Dad," Steven said with a laugh.

"How was your day, Dad?" Elizabeth asked.

Mr. Wakefield frowned. "To tell you the truth,

not so great, Liz. We've hired a new associate who really rubs me the wrong way. His name is Griffin Pierce, and he's one of these really aggressive, money-hungry young lawyers who will take on any case, as long as it earns him glamour and big bucks. Unfortunately, he's been assigned to me, so I'll be working pretty closely with him."

"I ought to interview this guy for my legal ethics project," Steven said. Recently Steven had been hard at work on an independent project for one of his courses at college. He wanted to become a lawyer in spite of what Mr. Wakefield had to say about the legal field.

"I wouldn't recommend that. Not unless you want to prove once and for all that *legal* and *ethics* are incompatible terms," Mr. Wakefield said.

"Maybe you should give up law to get away from this guy, Daddy," Jessica said with enthusiasm. "Do something new and fun. You could become an actor."

"Jessica, at my age, you don't just go and change what you do," he said firmly. His face had clouded over. "What could be keeping your mother? I'd hate to be late to the fund-raiser," he murmured.

Just then Mrs. Wakefield came hurrying out the side entrance of the office building. Her face was lit up with excitement. "Hi, everybody!" she cried, sliding into the front seat. She turned to Mr. Wakefield with a warm smile. "I didn't mean to keep you. Our meeting ran a few minutes over. We heard some pretty exciting news, too."

"What is it?" Mr. Wakefield asked, backing the car up and pulling out into traffic.

"You'll never believe what's happened. Remember I told you that the Valley Mall may be expanding? Well, it's definitely going to happen. They've already chosen the architects' design, and construction is due to begin any day. My firm is in the running for the contract to do all the interior design for the new wing!"

"Mom, that's wonderful," Jessica cried. "Does that mean it will be called the Alice Wakefield wing?"

Mrs. Wakefield laughed. "That's not terribly likely, Jess. But I'm excited about the chance to try out. This looks exactly like the kind of break our firm has been waiting for. Of course, our chances aren't that great. There will be at least four other firms competing, and some of them are very experienced. Still"—her eyes sparkled —"if we could do it, if we could get this contract . . ."

Mr. Wakefield pulled up at the civic center. "That's wonderful news, Alice. If anyone has a crack at it, you do." He shook his head admiringly. "You've really came a long way in your business, you know that? I'm proud of you."

"Thanks, dear. It makes me feel wonderful to know you're so supportive. I'm sorry you haven't been more excited about your own career lately—"

Mr. Wakefield cut her off. "Nonsense! I just hope something this exciting comes up for me one of these days, too."

"It will," Mrs. Wakefield said, leaning over and giving him a hug. "All right, everybody. Let's go in and give our support to Mr. Santelli," she added. "Something tells me he's going to be the next mayor!"

On Tuesday morning, when Jessica came downstairs to breakfast, she found Mrs. Wakefield sitting at the table with a cup of coffee and the morning paper.

"I can't believe it," she said as Jessica poured herself some orange juice. Mr. Wakefield, Elizabeth, and Steven came in as she spoke. "Everything was so wonderful at the campaign party last night, you'll never guess in a million years what's happened!"

"What?" Jessica asked.

"Mr. Santelli's been accused of accepting bribes as city planning commissioner." Mrs. Wake-

11

field shook her head. "I'm stunned. I can't imagine Peter ever doing anything against the law."

"There's no way Mr. Santelli would ever do anything illegal!" Elizabeth exclaimed. The party the night before had confirmed Elizabeth's sense that Mr. Santelli was a wonderful candidate for mayor. He'd always been a highly respected city official. They had all left the party full of excitement about the election.

Mr. Wakefield's face was pale. "That's absurd. Peter would never accept a bribe. Not in a million years. I can't imagine who could make an allegation like that."

"Neither can I," Mrs. Wakefield said, "but it's rotten timing. Even if the charges are dropped, one accusation can destroy a campaign."

"Well, it isn't over till it's over, Alice," Mr. Wakefield said. "Don't start assuming Peter's out of the race. It's exactly that kind of reasoning that will cost him votes."

Mrs. Wakefield looked surprised. "I wasn't—"

"It makes me so angry," Mr. Wakefield cut in, his expression darkening. "Peter's worked for this for years. And now one stupid lie could undo him. It isn't fair."

A moment of silence passed before Steven spoke up. "Well, listen," he said. "Maybe this is all just a terrible misunderstanding. I can't believe Mr. Santelli won't be able to clear his name. He's a wonderful candidate."

"I think so, too," Elizabeth agreed.

She picked up the newspaper. There was the story, right on the front page. "Mayoral Candidate Charged with Accepting Bribes!" the headline said. An "unidentified source" was cited. Elizabeth's stomach knotted up as she read the article.

Everything had seemed to be going right for Mr. Santelli the night before. The story couldn't be accurate. Elizabeth was convinced that there was absolutely no truth to the charges.

Two

"I can't wait to hear what everyone at school is saying about Maria's father," Jessica announced, climbing into the passenger seat of the Fiat Spider she shared with Elizabeth.

"Jessica, I'm sure Maria must be pretty upset about all this. The last thing she needs is to think people are talking about her."

Jessica sighed loudly. Elizabeth could be so unbelievably *good* sometimes, it drove her crazy!

"Well, I think it's interesting," she said in a sulky voice. "That's all. I mean, maybe Maria's father really *is* crooked. Wouldn't it be exciting if he were?"

Elizabeth shook her head. "Sometimes, Jess," she said, "your idea of what's exciting—"

"It isn't like he couldn't mend his ways," Jessica interrupted. "It could be just like this movie I saw on TV last week." She started filling Elizabeth in on the plot, which was so long and complicated, it took the rest of the way to school to tell it.

Elizabeth was still shaking her head when she got out of the car in the school parking lot. "Do me a favor, Jessica. Don't compare real life to the movies. I'm sure Maria won't want to hear about it." And before Jessica could say another word, Elizabeth had gone bounding off to greet Todd.

Jessica watched as her sister gave Todd a big hug. *Sometimes I can't believe we're twins*, she thought. She couldn't imagine being the sort of girl who really wanted to do her homework every night, who really wanted to waste every single weekend with the same boy, instead of going out with lots of different gorgeous guys. There was nothing really wrong with Todd. He was cute and nice, but Jessica thrived on change.

She hurried toward the school. She could hardly wait to find Lila Fowler and Amy Sutton, her two best friends, to hear what they had to say about the news!

"Everyone's talking about Maria," Lila said the minute Jessica found her and Amy in the hallway by their lockers. The only daughter of one of the richest men in Southern California, Lila loved excitement—and scandal. "That's it—he's finished. History," she added dramatically. "Done for."

16

"My mom thinks it's going to be the biggest story at the station," Amy confided. Mrs. Sutton worked for a local TV station. "She says unless Mr. Santelli can clear his name, there's no way he'll be able to win the election."

"Hey," Lila gasped, grabbing Jessica's arm. "There she is!"

They turned to watch Maria, who was walking down the hall alone, her face grave.

"Poor thing," Amy commented.

"It would've been so much fun knowing the mayor's daughter," Jessica said.

Lila shook her head. "I was even going to invite Maria over for dinner sometime soon, just to get to know her better." She shrugged. "I guess there's no reason to now."

Jessica and Amy nodded. Jessica had been bending over backward to be extra nice to Maria at cheerleading practice. Who could tell whether or not she would come in handy? Maybe Maria's father would've become governor of the whole state one day! Even as mayor he would have been a big celebrity. But Lila was right. There was no point in being friendly to Maria any longer. Chances were that they would never hear from Mr. Santelli again.

"Guess what?" Lila said in a bright voice. "Daddy's decided to buy me a present for my half-birthday. A video camera! Now I'll be able to make movies of all the famous people Daddy knows!''

Jessica couldn't believe it. It was bad enough that Lila had a car phone. This was too much.

Jessica was getting really tired of hearing her friend boast about her wealth, her father's friends, and all the things her father bought for her. Lila always had to be the first one to own a new gadget, the first one to spread the latest gossip. She had *everything*, and Jessica was sick of it! It was time for Jessica to come up with something new that Lila either didn't know about or didn't own.

Once again, on Wednesday evening, things didn't feel quite right to Elizabeth around the Wakefield house. The family didn't eat dinner together the way they usually did because both of her parents were staying late at the office. Elizabeth missed the warm gathering that usually accompanied her family's evening meal. She made herself a small salad, took it up to her room, and was just about to start on her history homework when her twin barged through the door. Normally she would have given Jessica a hard time for not knocking, but right now she was happy for the company.

"Hey," Jessica said, "are you busy?"

"Not really," Elizabeth said, immediately closing her history book.

"Guess what I just saw advertised on TV? It's this phone service for teenagers. You dial a nine hundred number and get to talk to all these other kids." Jessica's eyes were shining. "I'm dying to try it. They were interviewing this couple who met that way, and the guy was *so* gorgeous! And the girl talked about how romantic it was getting to know each other on the phone." She helped herself to some salad from Elizabeth's plate. "Kind of like love letters, only easier."

Elizabeth was used to her sister's enthusiasm for the latest fad, but this time she was concerned. "Those phone services cost a fortune," she told Jessica. "And I don't think it's a very good idea, anyway. You could meet some real creeps."

"Hey, you guys," Steven said, poking his head into Elizabeth's room. He was staying home the rest of the week to finish up some research for his legal ethics project. "Dad just got home. Let's go downstairs and keep him company. He's been kind of down since this whole Santelli scandal started."

So Steven's noticed, too, Elizabeth thought unhappily.

She followed her brother and sister downstairs to the front hallway, where Mr. Wakefield was hanging up his coat. He gave them a brief smile, but he looked drawn and pale.

"Hi, kids. Where's your mother?" he asked.

"Still not home," Jessica said.

"How was your day, Daddy?" Elizabeth asked quickly.

Before he could answer, the back door swung open, and they heard Mrs. Wakefield call, "Hi, everyone!"

"Hi, Mom," Elizabeth and Jessica said in unison.

Mrs. Wakefield walked to the front of the house to hang up her coat. "Why's everyone standing around in the hallway?" she asked.

"Dad just got home, too," Elizabeth said. "We were talking."

"Oh," Mrs. Wakefield said. "Has everyone eaten?"

"I ate downtown," Mr. Wakefield said. The twins and Steven said they had gotten their own dinners.

"Well, then," Alice Wakefield said, "any chance we can have coffee and dessert together?"

Within minutes coffee was brewing, and Elizabeth was dishing up chocolate ice cream for the whole family.

"Boy," Mrs. Wakefield said, kicking off her shoes and collapsing into a chair, "what a mess about Peter. It's all I've been hearing about for the past two days."

"Me, too," Steven said. "It seems like rumors are really spreading fast."

"Did you talk to Mr. Santelli today, Daddy?" Elizabeth asked.

"As a matter of fact, I did. I ran into him at a restaurant where we both go for lunch fairly often, and he sat down with me for a while. Naturally he was very upset. He insists that he's never accepted a bribe, and I have to tell you, I don't doubt it for a minute."

"What's he going to do?" Steven asked.

Mr. Wakefield shrugged. "I don't think he knows right now. Of course, he's still a candidate for mayor, and his first interest is in trying to minimize negative publicity. But you can imagine how hard that is to do. Meanwhile, police are investigating the matter. He told me they found that a huge sum of money was deposited into his bank account four days ago, but it was without his knowledge." Mr. Wakefield looked grim. "Ten thousand dollars. Can you imagine what'll happen once the papers get hold of that one?"

"How could the money have gotten there?" Elizabeth asked her father.

"Who knows? Someone could be framing him,

Liz." Mr. Wakefield sighed. "All I know is this: I think he's innocent."

"I agree," Mrs. Wakefield said fervently. "Poor Peter. It must be terribly frustrating for him after he's worked so hard."

Mr. Wakefield was quiet for a moment. "I think there's a lot more in store for him than frustration and disappointment. Because the police have uncovered this questionable bank deposit, I think we have to count on the fact that they will press criminal charges."

"What exactly does that mean?" Elizabeth asked.

"It means," her father said quietly, "that Mr. Santelli could be put on trial. And if he loses, he could be sent to prison."

Shocked silence followed these words. Elizabeth was still trying to find her voice when the phone rang. It was Mr. Santelli calling for Mr. Wakefield.

"Oh, no," Mr. Wakefield said sadly into the phone. "Peter, I'm so sorry." He was silent for a minute. "Well, I could meet you at your house tonight, but I'm afraid I'm not going to be much use to you in this one, Peter. I'm not a— I don't do that kind of law." After another brief pause, Mr. Wakefield cleared his throat. "Of course, Peter. I'll be right over."

"What happened?" Jessica asked the second her father hung up the phone.

"I'm afraid the worst has happened. Peter's been charged. He's out on bail now, but this thing is going to trial."

"Does he want you to defend him, Dad?" Steven asked.

Mr. Wakefield nodded. "He and I go way back. We've known each other for years, and I think he asked me to represent him because we're such old friends. He doesn't trust most of the lawyers he knows."

"Daddy, that isn't the only reason he asked you!" Elizabeth cried. "He asked you because he knows what a fantastic lawyer you are."

"That's right, Dad," Steven agreed. "Hey," he added, "why don't you do it? Why don't you take on his case and prove to whatever jerk is trying to frame him that it just won't work?"

"If I were your age again, Steven, with your optimism, maybe I could do that. But I haven't taken on a criminal case in fifteen years. I wouldn't even know where to begin," he added slowly.

Elizabeth sat straight up and stared at her father. "Dad, Steve's right. You *have* to do it. You're the only one who could save Mr. Santelli —and save his chance for becoming mayor."

Mr. Wakefield shook his head. "Now, wait a minute, Liz. I was just saying that I haven't—"

"That's a fantastic idea!" Jessica cried. "Dad, you'd be a hero! You'd probably get a big public appointment the minute he became mayor," she added.

"It's a ridiculous idea." Mr. Wakefield glanced at each member of his family. "But then, again—that doesn't make it a bad idea."

Mrs. Wakefield raised her brows. "Honestly, Ned, you're not really thinking of defending him, are you?"

"Why not?" he asked calmly.

"I know you've been disillusioned with work lately," Alice Wakefield said gently. "But wouldn't this just compound the problem? You'd probably have to work long hours," she added, "and right now, right after I've just taken on more responsibilities at the office, I'm not really sure—"

But Mr. Wakefield didn't seem to hear her. "You know," he interrupted, "I think you kids have a good point. There's no use sitting around and complaining about the way law works nowadays. It's up to me to try to do something to change it. After all, that's what I'm always telling you."

"Daddy," Elizabeth said excitedly, "does that mean you're going to take Mr. Santelli's case?"

Mr. Wakefield smiled. "Well, I'm certainly going to think about it," he said. "It may mean working a lot of extra hours, but I can't imagine anything more worthwhile!"

Elizabeth was delighted. She was sure this was exactly what her father needed. Once he saw how much good he could do for Mr. Santelli, he'd definitely take on the case. And she was sure he would win.

Jessica had had enough of the doom-and-gloom conversation her family was having. The first chance she got, she raced up the stairs to her room. She closed her door tightly and unfolded the slip of paper on which she had written the number of the party line she'd gotten from the TV commercial. She was so excited that she had butterflies in her stomach. "Romance! Excitement!" the ad had promised. "And all within easy reach. Just use your touch-tone phone." This was it. She had finally found something that Lila didn't know about and hadn't got to first. Jessica intended to take full advantage of that fact! She was going to find the most gorgeous, exciting boyfriend this way, and Lila would be green with envy. Jessica took a deep breath and punched the numbers. After a few rings, an operator answered.

"Would you like to be connected to the teen party line?" she asked.

"Yes, please," Jessica said.

The operator explained the rates, which Jessica didn't pay any attention to. "Fine, fine," she said. "Go ahead and put me through."

The next minute she heard a click, and then a bunch of voices.

"Hey!" a girl's voice said. "I think someone new has come on. Hello?"

"Hi," Jessica said.

"Hi. I'm Michael. Who are you?" a boy's voice said next.

Jessica introduced herself. There were six other people on the line. Four girls—Michelle, Sara, Nicola, and Bea—and two boys—Michael and Charlie.

"Where are you from, Jessica?" Charlie asked. She liked his deep, sexy voice. He definitely sounded cute.

"From Sweet Valley. What about you?"

"I'm from Riverdale," Charlie said, naming a nearby town.

"Hey, you two, this is a party line, remember?" Sara said in a coy, possessive voice.

Jessica felt her heart beat a little faster. This was definitely her kind of thing. Now she knew she had to compete with Sara for Charlie's attention, and there was nothing she liked more than going after what she wanted.

For the next ten minutes everyone joked

around, talking about school, shopping, surfing. Jessica made sure she got to pitch a few comments directly to Charlie, and she lingered over his name when she said goodbye.

"Hey, Jessica," he said, "will I get to talk to you again?"

"Maybe," Jessica said mysteriously. "I haven't decided yet."

"Oh, that voice. It's dazzling, Jessica. I can hardly wait to hear it again. Good night."

"Dazzling!" Jessica repeated to herself as she hung up. That was one of the nicest compliments anyone had ever given her. Charlie must be quite a guy, she thought. She could hardly wait to talk to him again. The party line was even better than she had thought it would be.

Three

On Thursday morning Mr. Wakefield was whistling when Elizabeth came down for breakfast. Mrs. Wakefield had already left for work.

"You sound cheerful today, Dad," Elizabeth commented.

"Good morning, sweetheart. Can I get you some juice?"

"Sure, thanks. So what happened last night at Mr. Santelli's?"

Mr. Wakefield removed a large carton of juice from the refrigerator. "Well, he convinced me defending him on this case would be the right thing to do. So I agreed to do it."

"Daddy, that's wonderful." She jumped up from her chair to give him a hug.

A few minutes later, the two of them left the house together. Jessica had gotten a ride to school with Lila that morning, so Elizabeth drove alone. She hummed all the way, pleased and excited about her father's decision to defend Mr. Santelli.

But the good mood around the Wakefield household didn't last for long. On Thursday evening Mr. Wakefield seemed tense about the possibility of a trial, rather than excited, and even worse, Elizabeth noticed that her parents were barely communicating. Mrs. Wakefield still didn't seem convinced that her husband's decision to defend Mr. Santelli was a good idea. And Mr. Wakefield was unhappy that Alice Wakefield had not gotten home until eight-thirty. Elizabeth had a feeling that meant things were only going to get worse.

It was all Elizabeth could think about at school on Friday. And it was still on her mind after school, when she and Todd met on the grassy lawn to talk about their days.

"Hey," Todd said, tipping up Elizabeth's chin and gazing deeply into her eyes, "I'd say 'penny for your thoughts,' but from your expression I have a feeling I ought to offer a little bit more. How about a buck?"

Elizabeth tried to smile, but it took a real effort. "Sorry, Todd. I'm just worried about my parents," she said softly.

"Your dad's still down in the dumps?" Todd asked sympathetically.

Elizabeth nodded. "I thought he was going to

start feeling better once he decided to defend Maria's father. But he's working harder than ever, and he seems to think it's a hopeless case. And in the meantime, my mom does nothing but work on her mall project."

"I guess that means they haven't had much time to be together," Todd said softly.

Elizabeth took a deep breath. "As far as I can tell, they've barely said two words to each other in the past two days. Mom is completely obsessed with this new project. And it's almost as if Dad is trying to compete with her by being as obsessed as she is! Todd, it's awful!"

Todd stroked the back of Elizabeth's neck. "You know what I'm worried about?" he asked thoughtfully. When Elizabeth didn't respond, he went on. "I'm worried about *you*. Because, as usual, you're worrying about everyone but yourself." His expression was tender and loving.

Elizabeth shook her head. "I don't know, Todd. I just keep thinking that there ought to be something I can do to relieve the tension around the house. But I can't think of anything."

"Liz! Hey, Elizabeth." Jessica came hurrying toward them across the green lawn with an urgent look on her face. "I've been looking for you everywhere," she cried, sitting down next to Elizabeth. "Cheerleading got canceled today, and I don't have a ride home. Can I take the Fiat?"

"And I thought you wanted to see me because you missed me so much after a whole day apart," Elizabeth joked. She dug in her pockets for the car keys. "Todd? Can I get a ride home with you?" When he nodded, she dropped the keys into her sister's outstretched hand.

"Hey, isn't it great having such a heroic father?" Jessica asked. "Maria was just telling me how great Dad is for coming to her father's rescue."

Elizabeth shrugged. "Remember what Dad said, Jess. It isn't going to be easy to disprove the bribery charge. The trial may drag on for ages. Besides," she added, "we don't want everyone expecting too much. If Dad loses, think how disappointed he'll be."

"He won't lose," Jessica said.

Elizabeth shook her head as she watched her twin dart off toward the parking lot. "Jessica is amazing," she said to Todd. "At first she seemed upset that Mom and Dad were arguing so much and about Daddy's attitude about his job. Now it doesn't seem to bother her at all."

"Maybe she has the right attitude," Todd said. "Things might just blow over. Every relationship goes through rough patches." He ran his fingers through her hair. "Even ours. That's what commitment is about—sticking together through the bad times as well as the good. Don't worry too much, Liz. Your parents will get through this just fine."

Elizabeth instinctively touched the gold locket Todd had given her a long time ago, when his father had been transferred to a new job in Vermont, and his whole family had moved away. True, she and Todd had weathered some rough times. They'd broken up, dated other people, and had still come back together. Elizabeth felt a tiny bit better. Once her parents got used to their new schedules, everything would be OK again.

She let herself relax as Todd slipped his arms around her and gave her a gentle kiss.

That evening Elizabeth was determined that the family was going to have a nice dinner together, even if it meant she had to make it. She stuck to a simple menu—hamburgers and salad—and her spirits rose as she finished each task. Todd was right. Everything was going to be just fine. She was worrying for no reason. Mr. Wakefield was in a good mood when he got home, full of stories about preparing for Mr. Santelli's trial. And the mood before dinner was much better than it had been over the past few days. Steven had gone out for dinner with his girlfriend, Cara Walker, the twins were both in high spirits, and they were having a good time joking around and teasing their father.

There was only one problem: Mrs. Wakefield didn't come home at six-thirty, the way she usually did. She didn't even come home by seven. Mr. Wakefield's good mood seemed to flatten a little, and finally, at ten past seven, he announced it was time for dinner.

"Shouldn't we wait for Mom?" Jessica asked.

Elizabeth shot her a look. *Tactful, Jess,* Elizabeth thought. *Very tactful.*

For the first five minutes or so no one said a word. The only sounds were the clinking of glasses and the sounds of forks tapping plates. Then suddenly the back door burst open, and Mrs. Wakefield rushed in, out of breath and looking very excited.

She stopped short when she saw they were all eating. "Oh, no! You poor things, you must have been famished," she gasped, setting down her briefcase, slipping out of her jacket, and sliding into her chair. "I'm so sorry, but we went into a meeting at five, and I couldn't get away. Not even long enough to make a phone call. But do you know what happened? We were meeting about the design project for the mall, and one of the decisions to be made was who should be in charge of the group running the project. They decided they want me to do it!"

"Mom, that's wonderful!" Elizabeth cried.

Jessica nodded enthusiastically. "Does that mean if your plan gets chosen they'll name the wing after you? Or do we at least get discounts from all the new stores?"

Mrs. Wakefield laughed. "I don't think so, Jess. But it does mean I'll be supervising the whole thing. We have to decide on the lighting, the colors, how the space will be used . . ." She stopped talking long enough to glance at her husband. "Ned, you haven't said anything."

Mr. Wakefield wiped his mouth carefully with his napkin. "Heading up the team sounds like even more work than being part of the team," he said quietly. "Isn't it going to mean awfully long hours? I'm sorry to say this, Alice, but right now—especially with my commitment to Mr. Santelli—is it really such a good idea for you to be taking on this much extra work?"

Mrs. Wakefield flushed. "It will mean some extra work, Ned, but this is the kind of project I've dreamed of for years! You know that."

Mr. Wakefield's mouth tightened. "Let's discuss this later, Alice," he said.

"There isn't anything to discuss," she said lightly. "I already told them I'd be happy to do it."

Dead silence fell over the table. Mr. Wakefield looked angry, but he didn't say anything.

"How was work today, Ned?" Mrs. Wakefield asked finally.

"Fine," he replied shortly.

Elizabeth felt miserable. Why had her mother agreed to take on the position without talking it over with her father? And why was her father being so unsupportive of her mother's wonderful achievement?

The tension in the air seemed to intensify when dinner ended and Mrs. Wakefield poured coffee. She thanked Elizabeth for making dinner, then turned to Jessica and said, "You might want to try to help your sister a little more now that your father and I are both going to be so busy."

"Thanks a lot," Jessica whispered to Elizabeth, shooting her twin a dirty look.

"Don't forget," Mrs. Wakefield said, "that we're all invited to go out on Doug Phelps's boat this Sunday." Doug Phelps was the senior partner in her design firm, and this outing was an important one.

Mr. Wakefield cleared his throat. "This Sunday? I thought it was next Sunday."

"You know it's this Sunday, Ned. And you know how important it is for us all to be there," Mrs. Wakefield added, sounding agitated.

"Well, I'm afraid I have a conflict. I told Peter Santelli that I'd spend the entire weekend working with him on preparing his defense. The trial is due to start on Monday," Mr. Wakefield said. Mrs. Wakefield looked surprised.

"You didn't tell me the trial was starting so soon." Her face looked pale. "At any rate, we have a commitment, Ned. It isn't going to look very good if we cancel out."

"*We* don't have to cancel out, *I* do," Mr. Wakefield said stubbornly. "Alice, you know how these things work. Peter is my client, and I have to respect his schedule. I can't just say we're not going to meet on Sunday because my wife wants to go boating!"

"Going boating," Mrs. Wakefield said coldly, "is not a fair way to describe what happens to be one of the most important social events my company has all year."

Angry silence filled the room, and Elizabeth kept her head down and stared at her plate. She hated hearing her parents argue.

"Well, I'm sorry, but you'll have to count me out on Sunday," Mr. Wakefield said in a quiet voice.

"That's just fine," Mrs. Wakefield snapped. Without another word, she stormed out of the room.

"Wow," Jessica said. "Mom sounds pretty mad."

Mr. Wakefield picked up his coffee cup. "Let's

just forget it," he said tersely. But it was hard to ignore the sound of the bedroom door slamming closed.

"Would you mind finishing up the dishes, Liz?" Jessica said at eight-fifteen, the appointed time for calling in to talk to Charlie. "I have some . . . uh, homework that I have to do."

Jessica felt a tiny bit guilty, but she couldn't keep Charlie waiting. And besides, she could hardly wait to talk to him!

She ran up to her room and quickly dialed the 900 number. Charlie was talking to Sara. "Have you heard the joke about the politician and the minister?" he asked her.

"No," Sara said, giggling in advance.

"Hi," Jessica cut in, making her voice sound as sultry as possible. "Charlie? It's me, Jessica."

Sara sounded annoyed. "Charlie's just telling me a joke. Go on, Charlie."

Charlie paused for a minute. "Actually, Sara, Jessica and I have . . . well, we have sort of a phone date. Don't we, Jessica?"

Sara snorted. "A phone date?"

"It's true," Jessica cut in. She loved the feeling of daring and intimacy the party line gave her. She also loved being flirtatious over the phone with a total stranger. "Hey," she asked

Charlie, "did you think about me today? Even once?"

"I thought about you without stopping. You were the substance of every breath I drew," Charlie announced.

Jessica giggled. "You're so . . . you talk so beautifully," she said.

"Charlie's a real poet," Sara chimed in. "That's why we all have crushes on him."

"To tell you the truth, I really am a poet," Charlie told Jessica. "In fact, I wrote you a poem today. But I'm too shy to read it to you—yet."

Jessica was completely charmed. A poet . . . on a teen talk line? What were the odds of that happening? Lila was going to be completely freaked out!

"I wish I could write *you* a poem," she said in a suggestive voice. "But I'm sure I can't write as beautifully as you."

"Jessica, from your voice . . . from your name . . . you *are* poetry," Charlie said.

This was too much. Here was this guy saying these incredible things to her—right in front of the others on the line!—and he hadn't even *seen* her yet. Jessica had always been convinced that her looks were about ninety-nine percent of the reason that guys asked her out. But Charlie couldn't see her. So why did he like her and not the others?

She was dying to find out. "Charlie," she said, "are you . . . I mean, when you heard my voice the first time I called, was there something in particular about me, or was it just . . . ? I don't know . . ."

She let her voice trail off. She loved the sense of letting her voice expose so much about her. She held her breath as she waited for Charlie's reply.

"I can't explain what happened, Jessica. All I know is, the minute I heard your voice I knew you were the one," Charlie said solemnly.

Jessica felt her cheeks get hot. This guy was terrific. If he was this great to talk to on the telephone, she could just imagine how wonderful he'd be in person!

Four

The weekend had passed quickly, but by Monday morning Elizabeth could hardly remember the last time her parents had spent five minutes together. She and Jessica has accompanied their mother on the boat outing on Sunday, minus their father. On Monday evening Mrs. Wakefield had set up a temporary office in one corner of the living room, since Mr. Wakefield needed the den for working on *his* project. It was hard not to notice the fact that work was intruding on their family life.

The mall project was all that Alice Wakefield could talk about. It was clear that this project was the turning point in her career. If her firm won the competition and actually got to design the new wing of the mall, she would be the one in the limelight, since she was in charge of the whole thing. This would open up all sorts of opportunities for her in the future. Mrs. Wakefield had never really designed the interior of such a large public space, and this could mean the beginning of a wonderful stream of jobs.

"It's funny," she confided on Tuesday night at dinner. "But so much of what designers have to do to earn a living these days is purely functional. It's a real challenge to have a public space of this size to work with. The whole job is so exciting. I really feel we can do it, too, that we can win the competition."

"That's great, Mom," Elizabeth commented. "I have a feeling you're going to win." She noticed that her father didn't even respond. In fact, he never seemed to want to talk about Mrs. Wakefield's mall project. He rushed through his meal, then went into his study to do some more work for the trial.

Elizabeth couldn't even confide in Jessica about her concern. These days, her twin was wandering around the house as if she were walking on air. A few weeks before, Jessica had been extremely worried about the increasing number of arguments her parents were having. But now, Elizabeth noticed, Jessica seemed to be totally oblivious to the fact that things around the Wakefield house had taken a dramatic turn for the worse, especially since Mr. Santelli's trial had begun the day before. Now both the Wakefield parents were stressed out, frantically busy, and completely on edge.

Elizabeth had noticed that her father had started giving different versions of stories about work to her mother than he gave to her and Jessica.

The night before, for example, when her father had come home—finding only Jessica and Elizabeth, of course—he had confided that he thought Mr. Santelli's trial was going to be really tough. First there was the problem of the money that had been deposited in Mr. Santelli's account. Peter claimed he knew nothing about it, but there the money was. Who had put it there? How could they get a lead? Even worse, the police claimed to have come up with other incriminating evidence against the defendant. Mr. Wakefield was sure Mr. Santelli was honest, but proving that in court was another matter altogether. The fact that Mr. Santelli was still running for mayor just raised all the stakes. It meant more publicity and more pressure. And it was beginning to appear that it would be a hard case to settle.

As soon as Mrs. Wakefield had gotten home and asked about the trial, Mr. Wakefield's tune had changed completely. He had told her that it was going great, that all his preparatory work had really paid off, that it looked like an easy acquittal.

"Really?" Mrs. Wakefield had said, looking surprised. "I would've thought it would be pretty difficult, especially with that issue of the deposit in his bank account."

"Well, that isn't the case at all," Mr. Wakefield had said tersely.

"If only they'd talk to each other!" Elizabeth moaned now to her twin. They were in Jessica's room, and Jessica was lying flat on her back on her bed, staring up at the ceiling. "Don't they have any idea what they're doing, that they're just moving further and further apart from each other—just when they need to be closest?"

Jessica sat up with effort. "Liz," she said calmly, "try to stop hyperventilating. At first I thought it was terrible that they were arguing so much and both had so much to do, but things have been pretty blissful around here." She grinned. "With Mom so busy I don't even have to clean up my room anymore." She pointed to the mountain of clothes piled up on her desk chair. Elizabeth noticed that the room did look messier than usual. "I can come home whenever I want," Jessica went on. "She lets us each get our own dinner so we don't have to start dinner anymore. Plus neither one of them seems to care that I've been using this party line every night." Jessica flopped back down on her bed. "Kind of a great arrangement, if you ask me."

"Don't you think that's a little selfish?"

Jessica shrugged. "Mom and Dad know how to take care of themselves, silly. So what if they get a little tense with each other from time to time? It's not exactly like the world's falling apart, Liz. Why don't you just calm down and take it easy?"

Elizabeth couldn't help getting aggravated. "That's easy for you to say. When was the last time you went to the grocery store—or even fed Prince Albert?"

Jessica propped herself up on her elbows and glared at her twin. "Nobody's telling you that you have to do that stuff, Liz. You just go ahead and do it, and then you get mad at people! Well, you can't blame me if I'm managing to have a good time anyway."

Elizabeth was about to make an angry retort when she realized that she and her sister were fighting now, too. "Never mind," she muttered. "I didn't mean to snap at you, Jess."

"That's OK," Jessica said blithely. "Now, if you don't mind, I have a phone call to make. It's private."

Elizabeth wandered back into her own room. Right then she would have given anything to be her twin sister—to be able to see the change in the family as nothing more than a chance for additional freedom.

But that wasn't the way it felt to Elizabeth at all.

That night there was a new boy on the party line.

Jessica hadn't realized how quickly a feeling of community had developed among the regulars. By now everyone knew that something was going on between Jessica and Charlie. Michael took turns flirting with Nicola and Bea, and Sara just seemed to get upset and feel sorry for herself and interrupt all the good conversations.

That evening the conversations were going particularly well. Luckily Sara was bothering Michael and Nicola for a change, and Bea was fairly quiet, leaving Jessica and Charlie to talk just to each other.

"How're you doing, gorgeous? I've been thinking about you all day long," Charlie said.

Jessica's heart skipped a beat. "I'm fine," she said, twisting the telephone cord as she talked. That was how her tongue felt when she talked to Charlie—twisted! She wished she could be as clever and spontaneous as he was.

"I've been building a mental picture of you today," Charlie continued. "I've decided—just from your voice—that you're blond. Am I right?"

Jessica giggled. "You're right," she confessed.

"I could tell," Charlie said triumphantly. "You have the blondest voice I've ever heard."

Jessica felt shivers of delight go through her. Imagine how thrilled Charlie was going to be when he discovered just how blond she really was! She tried to imagine what it would be like when she and Charlie finally met. He probably thought she was sort of cute, or maybe even on the plain side. Jessica was sure there was *no way* he could think that she looked the way she really did. Jessica imagined their first meeting on the beach. Naturally it would be deserted, except for the two of them coming closer and closer. He would stare at her and say, in that wonderful husky voice of his, "Are you really Jessica? You're like a dream come true." Then they would fall into each other's arms and kiss—deeply and passionately.

"And blue eyes, right?" Charlie continued.

"Bluish," she revised. No point in spoiling the surprise by admitting that her eyes were as blue-green as the ocean, framed by long, thick lashes. There had to be *some* surprises for Charlie!

He cleared his throat. "As for height," he murmured, "I don't think you're too tall, princess. But not too short either. Five-five, that's my guess."

"Five-six!" Jessica cried with delight. Was Charlie psychic? He seemed to have guessed exactly what she looked like.

What about her? Had she guessed what Charlie looked like?

The funny thing was, until now she really hadn't thought about it. She listened to his warm, sexy voice for a moment and decided that naturally he was gorgeous. He probably had dark curly hair, maybe brown with some golden highlights. And warm brown eyes with little glints of green in them. And—

She was just about to tell Charlie some of her ideas about his appearance when someone new cut in.

"Hello? Is this the teen line? Did I get the right number? My name is Earl Wasserman," he announced.

The conversation that had been going on between Michael, Sara, and Nicola stopped, and Jessica and Charlie were quiet, too. Jessica was a little annoyed at the intrusion, but she knew that wasn't fair. Hadn't she broken in on the others just a week ago?

"How does this work?" Earl asked. "Do we all just talk at the same time? I saw the ad on TV and really wanted to try it," he explained with a nervous laugh. "Does it really cost a whole dollar a minute?"

A dollar a minute? Jessica couldn't believe her ears. Was that possible? She'd been on the phone as much as thirty minutes a night!

"Wow," she said to Charlie, "that's a fortune. Is that really what it costs?"

"Princess," Charlie said in a teasing voice, "don't you know that you're worth a zillion times that?"

Jessica swallowed hard. She could hardly tell him that she wasn't sure her parents would feel the same way. She just hoped the two of them stayed as busy and distracted as they'd been for a while. Maybe by some miracle they would never notice.

"When I said I wanted to do something special, this wasn't exactly what I had in mind." Todd teased Elizabeth on Wednesday, stopping next to her in the frozen food section of the supermarket while she consulted her list.

"Ice cream. Daddy loves this flavor," she announced, taking two pints out of the freezer. "Sorry, Todd," she added, leaning over to give him a quick kiss on the cheek. "But I don't know who else would go out and get food this week if I didn't. My mother's up to her chin in work for this competition. And my dad's just as bad, now that the trial is really under way."

"How's the trial going? Has he said?"

"Well, there are two different versions," Elizabeth admitted, moving the cart up the aisle. "When he talks to us about it—Jessica and me—he sounds pretty dispirited. I get the impression there just isn't enough to go on so far to be able to clear Mr. Santelli's name. And no one at the bank has been much help, either. My sense from my father is that the judge may just dismiss the whole case, claiming lack of sufficient evidence."

"That wouldn't exactly do Mr. Santelli much good," Todd commented.

"Right. But when my father's telling my mom about the trial, you'd think he was talking about a completely different event! He keeps telling her it's going perfectly, that his defense has been great." Elizabeth sighed. "I can understand why he's doing this, but it worries me just the same. He ought to be able to turn to her for help right now. And instead, he feels like he has to make himself look like a hero."

"That's hard," Todd commiserated softly. "But at least you know you're doing everything you possibly can to help them both."

Elizabeth nodded. She *did* know that. She just hoped it was going to make a difference.

*   *   *

When Elizabeth got home with the groceries, she was surprised to see her mother's car parked in the driveway. It was the first day in weeks Mrs. Wakefield had been home before dark.

"Mom?" she called as she came into the kitchen carrying two bags of groceries.

"In here, Liz. I'm on the phone," her mother called from the den.

Elizabeth started slowly unpacking the food. Her mother's voice drifted out from the den, and Elizabeth could hear her discussing the plans for the mall's new wing. Her mother sounded different—so authoritative, so sure of herself! Like an executive, Elizabeth thought.

Then Mrs. Wakefield hung up the phone and came into the kitchen. "Liz! I was going to go to the store tomorrow," she exclaimed, looking guiltily at the bags of food on the counter that Elizabeth was unpacking. "How did you pay for all this?"

"I used our charge at the store," Elizabeth said. "I didn't know you were planning to go later," she added slowly. "Maybe I should've just waited. . . ."

"No, no. Thanks, dear. You're a wonderful help," Mrs. Wakefield said, helping her daughter unpack the second bag. "I've really appreciated everything you've been doing around the house lately, Liz. I can't tell you how important this project is to me and how much it means to me that I know I have my children's support."

She gave Elizabeth a big smile. What could Elizabeth say after that? She could hardly complain that they had barely seen her in the past couple of weeks.

"Listen," Elizabeth said, "it'll be worth it if this all comes through and you become a famous designer." She gave her mother a smile. "Then we can get back to normal again around here," she added pointedly.

Mrs. Wakefield didn't answer. She just continued unpacking groceries, a distracted expression on her face, as if she hadn't even heard what Elizabeth had said.

Five

For the rest of that week, Elizabeth felt that the situation was improving. Both her parents were just as absorbed as they had been in what they were doing, but Elizabeth noticed that there was a feeling of shared hard work between them. In fact, Mr. Wakefield gave her mother a hug on Friday night. "Let's make sure we go out tomorrow night—just the two of us—and catch a movie." It made Elizabeth feel great when she heard her mother agree.

On Saturday afternoon Mr. Wakefield left the house around one o'clock to run some errands. For several hours Mrs. Wakefield worked on the project, until a phone call came that seemed to cause her some frustration. After she hung up, she gathered some papers together and reached for her briefcase. It was almost four o'clock, and Mr. Wakefield still wasn't back.

"Darn," Mrs. Wakefield said, glancing at her

watch and then turning to her daughters. "Your father and I had talked about going to see a movie tonight, but it doesn't look like it's going to work out. When he gets home, tell him I had to go back to the office. OK?"

Don't go, Elizabeth pleaded silently. *Or at least write him a note yourself. Please Mom.* But she didn't dare say anything. Her mother was already slipping into her jacket and scooping up her briefcase, her expression distracted.

"See?" Elizabeth said, giving her sister a look when their mother had gone outside. "I told you, Jess. It's getting worse."

Jessica opened the refrigerator and took out an apple. "Oh, Liz, don't be such a worrywart. Mom and Dad can go to the movies together anytime. It's no big deal." She took a bite of apple. "Hey, by the way, did I tell you Steve called this afternoon? He's coming home tomorrow to cover the rest of Dad's trial for his ethics project."

Elizabeth felt her mood lighten. "He is? That's wonderful!" she exclaimed. having Steven around for the next few days might improve the mood around the house.

"Liz," Jessica continued, "what do you think of my voice? Do you think I sound kind of sexy or more on the coy, flirtatious side?"

Elizabeth stared at her sister. "Hey, forgive

me for not seeing the connection, but what does that have to do with anything, Jessica? Your voice sounds exactly the way it always does."

Jessica gave her an insulted look. "Come on, Liz. Just answer me."

Elizabeth continued to scrutinize her. "Does this have anything to do with this telephone party line you've been talking on?" she asked.

"Maybe," Jessica said. "Come on, Liz, tell me the truth. I'm trying to find out how you think I'd sound to a total stranger. Do I sound sixteen, or older? Do you think I sound like someone you'd want to get to know better?" she added anxiously.

"Jessica," Elizabeth said sternly, crossing her arms, "have you met someone on this phone line? Because I should tell you right now I don't think it's a very good idea for people to meet that way. Absolutely anyone could call in, just from seeing the ad on TV. You have no idea what kind of creeps could be using the telephone as a chance to meet girls." She frowned at her sister. "Promise me you won't agree to meet anyone from the phone line."

Jessica's eyes flashed. "Who do you think you are, my mother?" she snapped. "The fact is, I *have* met someone nice on the phone line. And he isn't a creep or a weirdo or anything else. He's a perfectly nice guy, and I have every intention of meeting him in person."

Elizabeth frowned. "Well, I still don't think it's a very good idea. I may not be your mother, but I *am* your sister. And even if you don't care what happens to you, I do. I don't think you're being very smart, Jess." She shook her head. "And you're probably running up the biggest phone bill we've ever had."

"OK, Miss Wakefield," Todd said in a teasing voice, "are you going to come down to Planet Earth and let me treat you to the best dinner a guy on a strict budget can afford?"

Elizabeth laughed. She and Todd were having Chinese food on Sunday evening, a special treat—and all the more special since the situation at home was still chaotic. Steven was helping Mr. Wakefield get some briefs ready for the trial the next day, and Mrs. Wakefield was at a meeting. "Do you know how wonderful it is to see you?" Elizabeth asked Todd wistfully, her eyes fixed on his.

It was amazing to her how supportive he'd been over the past few weeks. Elizabeth could tell Todd anything, and he would understand. If it hadn't been for him, and her best friend, Enid Rollins, Elizabeth really thought she might have fallen apart.

Now Elizabeth told Todd how upset her father had been the night before when Mrs. Wakefield canceled their movie date. "It was terrible," she confided. "Todd, he got so mad when I told him! At first I thought he was mad at me, then he apologized later. He was just so disappointed."

Todd covered her hand with his. "That's rough," he said softly.

Elizabeth nodded. "I wish you and I could have gotten together last night," she added. Todd had gone to a basketball game with his father, and she had missed him.

"Well, let's make up for it tonight," Todd said softly, leaning closer to her.

Despite the cheerful buzz around them in the restaurant, Elizabeth felt as if she and Todd were completely alone. Gradually she felt herself relaxing, enjoying her meal, settling into the private world she and Todd had built around them. She really hated for the evening to end.

"Let me walk you to the door," Todd said when he drove her home later.

"You should get going," Elizabeth demurred. "I know you have a lot of homework to do tonight. I can make it up the front walk myself."

"No way. I want to be gallant," Todd insisted, turning off the engine, getting out of the car, and opening her door for her. Elizabeth wrapped her arm tightly around Todd's waist as they sauntered up the front walk. Todd gave her a lingering kiss at the door.

"You're amazing," she whispered, tightening her arms around his neck and gazing up into his eyes. "Do you know how much I love you?"

"I love you, too," Todd whispered, bending over to press one tiny fluttering kiss on each of her cheeks. "Now, promise me you won't worry about a thing. Go straight upstairs, hop into bed, and have sweet dreams till I see you again in the morning."

Elizabeth laughed. "I promise," she said softly.

She opened the door and stepped into the foyer. Immediately she heard angry voices coming from the den.

"I'm sick and tired of this, Alice. We haven't had dinner together as a family in ages. You're never home, and when you are home, you're working. What kind of life is this?"

Her father sounded furious. And Mrs. Wakefield's retorts were just as sharp, just as angry.

Elizabeth felt all the joy from her evening with Todd rush out of her. Her eyes filled with tears. It was such a rude shock, coming home from a wonderful time . . . to this.

She didn't even bother telling her parents she was home. She just ran straight upstairs to her bedroom. Closing her door behind her, she burst into tears.

For a moment tonight, she had believed that everything was going to be fine again. But that belief had been shattered. The only solid thing she had to hang on to was Todd.

What was happening to her family?

"Jessica," Amy Sutton said, "have you ever thought that it might be time for you to settle down and get yourself a boyfriend? I just read an article in the latest *Ingenue* that claims that playing the field is passé. It's time for commitment, they said."

The girls were lounging upstairs in Jessica's room on Sunday evening. In the old days, Jessica thought with satisfaction, she wouldn't have been allowed to have a friend over this late on a school night. But her parents had been so absorbed in work this afternoon and evening that no one had objected when she'd asked if she could have Amy over. Steven was over at Cara's house, and she had no idea where Elizabeth was. Probably doing all the household chores for the next week.

"I *have* met a guy, for your information," Jessica said coolly. "I don't know if he's commitment material, but he's pretty great."

"Where's he from? How come I haven't seen him?" Amy demanded.

Jessica shrugged. "Well, because he's—hidden," she concluded with a mysterious smile.

"What do you mean, 'hidden'? Is he for real or isn't he?" Amy looked doubtful. "I don't believe you've really met someone," she said at last. "Hidden or otherwise. I think you've just run out of guys at school, and now you're stuck having to invent them."

Jessica was indignant. "You want to bet? I *have* met a guy—a great guy. His name is Charlie," she added.

Amy still looked unsure, and Jessica decided this was the time to let out her secret. "I'll tell you what. Go down to the kitchen and pick up the extension so you can listen in. I'm calling Charlie right now."

Amy gave her a strange look. "OK," she said, still dubious.

Jessica dialed the teen party line number. A minute later she heard the click as the operator put her through, and Amy picked up the phone in the kitchen.

"Hi, guys. It's Jessica," she announced.

"What took you so long to call? I've been dying to talk to you," Charlie said.

"Oh, I was kind of held up here. I have a friend over. In fact, she's on the line now. Ame? You can talk," Jessica said.

"Uh . . . hi, Charlie."

"Another person!" Sara cried.

Amy cleared her throat. "How many people are on this line, anyway?"

"Listen, any friend of Jessica's is a friend of mine," Charlie said warmly. "Did Jessica mention to you that I happen to be nuts about her, or did she leave that part out?"

This was perfect! Jessica thought. Amy would have to crawl on her hands and knees, apologizing, for not having believed her!

They didn't stay on the phone for long, but Jessica promised Charlie she would call back the next night. "Don't wait so long tomorrow night," he begged her. "I was really afraid I'd miss you tonight."

"Wow, Jess," Amy said, wide-eyed, coming back into her friend's bedroom after they had hung up the phones. "How did you get in on this thing? Do you know who these people are?"

"Not really. I mean, I know who Charlie is. At least, I know I like him," Jessica said. She shivered. "Isn't it romantic? It's like having a secret admirer or something."

"You mean you two haven't met yet? And he's saying that he's crazy about you?" Amy shook her head. "That seems a little weird to me. How do you know he isn't a maniac?"

"Why would he be a maniac?" Jessica asked

crossly. "Listen, Amy, can't you be a little happier for me? I happen to be really nuts about this guy. He's fantastic. Can't you hear it in his voice? He's funny, he's warm, he's sweet . . ." Her voice trailed off. "And I can just tell how sexy he is, too."

Amy shrugged. "Well, I don't know how you can tell that just from the telephone. Aren't you planning on ever meeting?"

Jessica thought about that for a moment. "Yeah," she said at last. "We're going to meet. In fact, I'm going to suggest to him that we meet soon, like this coming week." She looked dreamily at her friend. "Aren't you jealous, Ame? By this weekend I'll be out strolling along the beach with Charlie . . . driving up to Miller's Point. . . ."

"I don't know, Jess. I wouldn't get my hopes up if I were you. All you've heard is a voice. There's no telling what this guy Charlie is really like."

Jessica moaned. "You're hopeless," she cried. "Absolutely hopeless. You don't have an ounce of romance in your soul. And another thing, don't tell Lila about this," she commanded. "I want to be the one to surprise her once Charlie and I are the hottest new couple around!"

Six

"It isn't like you to be so down, Liz," Enid said at lunch on Monday. Enid had been Elizabeth's closest friend for years, and she knew Elizabeth well enough to be able to say what she thought. "I know how hard it must be for you at home. But I think Todd's right. I think couples go through lots of ups and downs, and your parents are probably just going through some turbulence right now." She shook her head. "You know how sympathetic I am to this stuff," she added. Enid's parents had separated years ago, and she knew better than most people what it felt like to watch a family come apart. "But don't start thinking your parents are doomed to split up just because things have been a little tense!"

Elizabeth sighed. "Maybe you're right, Enid. Anyway, a lot of this stuff is bound to get better soon. My mother's supposed to find out today or tomorrow whether or not her firm's been chosen to design the mall. Once we know for sure, some of the tension will go away."

"Of course it will," Enid said reassuringly. "And I'm sure your father's trial won't go on forever, either."

Elizabeth nodded. "That's true," she said softly. "You know, maybe I *have* been too down lately. Maybe all my parents need is some humor and comfort when they get home." Her eyes brightened. "I know. I'll make spaghetti and meatballs with a special sauce for them tonight as a surprise! And I can make garlic bread and a big salad, too."

"That's the spirit," Enid said warmly. "They probably *do* need a little extra warmth and support. And I bet a big family dinner is exactly the right thing to plan!"

Elizabeth felt much better for the rest of the day. During an after-school meeting of the newspaper staff, she scribbled down a list of things she would need, and Todd agreed to help her do the shopping after school.

By five-thirty, they had finished shopping, and Todd dropped Elizabeth off at home, giving her a warm hug first. Elizabeth tried to keep her spirits up when she unlocked the front door. The house was empty, and Prince Albert was jumping up and down, wildly excited to see her.

"Poor little Prince," Elizabeth murmured affectionately, snapping the leash onto the dog's collar and taking him outside for a walk.

An hour later a wonderful tomato-and-mushroom sauce was bubbling away on the stove. Elizabeth set the dining room table with her favorite tablecloth, even putting out candles for a festive touch. It looked perfect!

"What's this?" Jessica demanded when she got home. She wandered into the kitchen and jabbed one finger into the tomato sauce bubbling on the stove. "This is yummy. Liz, I have to say one thing. Since Mom's been so obsessed with this mall project, your cooking skills have improved!"

"Thanks," Elizabeth said dryly. "Look," she added, "I really want to make this a family meal tonight, Jess. Can you try and stick around for the whole meal and not disappear on me? I want Mom and Dad to feel like we're all . . . you know . . ."

"One big happy family?" Jessica asked innocently.

Elizabeth laughed. "Mind reader."

Just then the back door opened, and Mr. Wakefield and Steven came in. They both looked utterly exhausted. Mr. Wakefield loosened his tie, not even noticing that Elizabeth had prepared dinner. "Hi, girls," he said in a tired voice. "I'm going upstairs to wash up. I'll be down in a minute."

"What's wrong with him?" Jessica demanded, turning to her brother after Mr. Wakefield had left the room.

Elizabeth felt herself getting anxious. "Is it the trial? Did something go wrong?"

"The judge suspended the case," Steven explained. "Basically he decided that there wasn't enough evidence one way or the other—just what Dad thought might happen. He's crushed, though," Steven said sadly, running one hand through his hair. "He feels it's his fault. He's blaming himself for throwing Mr. Santelli's career away."

"That's ridiculous!" Elizabeth said. "For one thing, Mr. Santelli hasn't lost his chance of being mayor yet. He's still in the running. And for another—"

"Shhh," Jessica whispered, putting a finger to her lips. "He's coming back downstairs."

Elizabeth poked unhappily at her spaghetti sauce. Why was it she had a feeling that her wonderful family dinner wasn't going to be enough to lift her father's spirits?

"I suppose Steve's told you the bad news,"

he said quietly as Elizabeth placed the spaghetti into boiling water.

Both girls nodded. "Dad, I think it's awful. I don't understand how the case can just be thrown out," Elizabeth said.

"Well, as I think I've been saying for days now, this case was difficult. The judge decided the prosecuting attorney's evidence—namely, the money deposited in Peter's account and the unidentified source that claimed Peter accepted bribes—wasn't strong enough. By the same token, there wasn't enough to go on to clear Peter's name." Mr. Wakefield looked disconsolate. "I just feel that it's all my fault. We can try for a retrial, see if there's any other way to clear Peter's name, but right now it's pretty hopeless."

"Well," Jessica said brightly, "I'm sure you tried your hardest, Daddy. And I'm sure Mr. Santelli is glad you went to so much trouble for him."

"I wish I were so sure," Mr. Wakefield said gloomily. A long silence filled the air. "Where's your mother?" he asked, a bitter note in his voice. "It's almost seven o'clock."

"Let's just have some iced tea out on the patio and wait for her," Elizabeth jumped in, trying to stave off the fight she feared was coming.

"All right," Mr. Wakefield said.

Time seemed to creep by while they were waiting for Mrs. Wakefield. Mr. Wakefield didn't want to talk about the trial, except to reprimand himself for what he considered to be a disastrous job. No one really knew what to say, and the sound of the clock ticking loudly didn't help.

"Hey," Jessica said to Elizabeth. "When did you put the spaghetti in? Shouldn't it be done by now?"

"Oh, no!" Elizabeth cried, jumping up and racing into the kitchen. Sure enough, the pasta had been boiling so long, it had turned into a gluey mess. She held up a forkful. "It's ruined," she said miserably.

"Well, let's see about making something else," her father said in a curt voice, coming into the kitchen behind her and opening the freezer. "We're not waiting for your mother a minute longer. Let's put some of these frozen dinners in the microwave."

Elizabeth felt her eyes fill with tears. She'd had such high hopes, and now her wonderful dinner was spoiled.

"I don't know if these are any good, Daddy," Jessica was saying skeptically, turning over one of the frozen packages.

"Just put them in the microwave and let's eat some dinner!" her father snapped.

"Dad," Elizabeth said, "it won't take long to cook more spaghetti—if we have any." She opened one of the cupboard doors. The shelves were almost bare.

"Hi, everyone!" Mrs. Wakefield said cheerfully as she opened the kitchen door. She was holding a bottle of champagne. "Guess what!" she cried. "We did it. We got the project!" She twirled around the kitchen, setting down the bottle and engulfing the twins in a warm embrace. "Can you believe it? Your mother is going to be in charge of the group that won the competition to design the interior of the new west wing of Sweet Valley Mall!"

Shocked silence greeted this news. Mr. Wakefield stared at her, still holding the frozen dinners.

"Ned, I'm so happy!" Mrs. Wakefield cried, throwing her arms around him.

"You may be happy," he said coldly, "but you're also extremely late, Alice. Liz made dinner for you and tried to keep it, and the fact is, it got ruined. If you're not considerate enough to come home for dinner, couldn't you at least call?"

The look of joy and exuberance vanished from Mrs. Wakefield's face, and she looked questioningly at her husband. "You sound pretty upset," she said slowly, as if she were trying to

69

get her balance back. "Is anything wrong? How's the trial going?"

Mr. Wakefield made an exasperated sound. "It's all over, Alice. The judge threw out the case today for lack of sufficient evidence, and lack of sufficient defense. It looks as if Peter's political career is all over, washed up." He sighed.

Mrs. Wakefield bit her lip. "I guess this wasn't very good timing," she said slowly. "I didn't mean to rush in here blurting out my good news. I'm sorry, Ned."

For a full minute no one said a word. Mr. Wakefield stared at Mrs. Wakefield, expressionless. "Well," he said at last, "you must be very excited." His words came out so flatly, Elizabeth's heart sank. Couldn't he be happy for her mother?

"I—well, I am, Ned," Mrs. Wakefield said in a soft voice.

Mr. Wakefield cleared his throat. "I take it that means we'll be seeing even less of you around here from now on than we have these past couple of weeks," he said gruffly.

Mrs. Wakefield turned pale. Then, clearing her throat, she said calmly, "I hope we'll get things under control fairly quickly. But it's a huge project, Ned. You know that. I'm asking my staff to work extraordinary hours, and you

70

know it wouldn't be fair unless I was willing to work there with them. I would've hoped," she added, "that you'd be happy for me."

Mr. Wakefield's eyes flashed with anger. "I am," he said. "I'm glad you've gotten what you wanted, Alice." And before she could say another word, he stormed out of the kitchen, leaving everyone else staring after him in alarm.

"Well," Mrs. Wakefield said uncertainly, staring at the bottle of champagne in front of her, "I guess maybe we should see about getting those frozen dinners cooked."

Elizabeth stared disconsolately at the pot of sauce still sitting on the stove. So much for a wonderful family meal.

Seven

"Look, Mom!" Jessica exclaimed at breakfast the next morning, passing the newspaper across the table. "You're famous!"

Mrs. Wakefield blushed. "Did they put something in the paper about our firm?" she asked, leaning over for a better look. Sure enough, in the second section of the paper, there was a short piece about the design project. "The new wing will be planned by a team headed by Alice Wakefield," the article announced.

"What's that?" Mr. Wakefield asked, coming into the kitchen and pouring himself some coffee.

"Oh, nothing," Mrs. Wakefield said quickly, closing the newspaper and getting to her feet. "Can I get you some coffee or a muffin?" she asked solicitously.

Mr. Wakefield shook his head. "I'm running late as it is. I should get to the office." He cleared his throat. "Well, you have a good day,

Alice. Enjoy the fruits of success, as they say. You worked hard, you deserve to ride the crest for a few days."

"It won't be any different," Mrs. Wakefield said dismissively.

Mr. Wakefield shrugged. "Fine. Anyway, I'll see you this evening." And with that he took his briefcase and left.

"Mom," Jessica protested, "you didn't even show Daddy the article in the paper!"

Mrs. Wakefield cocked her head to make sure her husband was out of earshot. "Your father is really down about the trial, sweetheart. I don't think it's going to make him feel great if I keep going on and on about winning the design project. In fact, I think it would be a good idea if we all tried our hardest to downplay it."

Jessica looked disappointed. "You're famous, Mom. Why should we downplay anything?"

"Jessica, please. I'm not famous. And you never know how these things go. If the owners of the mall don't like our plans, they can still reject them."

Elizabeth helped herself to some cereal. "Maybe it would make Dad feel better if he knew more about the design project, not less," she said slowly.

Mrs. Wakefield frowned. "I don't think so, Liz. Your father needs attention right now, attention focused on him, not on me. As I said, I'd really prefer not to talk about this too much."

Elizabeth was confused. Was this really the best way to approach the situation? It seemed to her that a lot of the problem came from the fact that her parents hadn't been sharing much in each other's lives.

Still, it wasn't up to her to give her mother advice. Elizabeth sighed heavily and took a small bite of cereal. She just hoped her mother knew what she was doing.

"You're home early," Elizabeth said that afternoon when the back door opened and her father came in. Mr. Wakefield didn't even look at Elizabeth. He walked straight through the kitchen, set down his briefcase, and went upstairs, all without a word. Steven, who had the rest of the week to write up his independent study project, came in right behind his father.

"What's wrong?" Elizabeth demanded, turning to her brother.

"Everyone at Dad's office was talking about the judge's decision to dismiss Santelli's case. The trial is the talk of the town, which is exactly what Dad was dreading. All this talk leaves Mr. Santelli even worse off than he was before. His name hasn't been cleared, he's been dragged through a public trial, and now there's definitely scandal associated with his name."

"Oh, no," Elizabeth said. "Dad must be really mad!"

Steven shook his head. "No. That's the weird thing. I don't think he's angry at anyone but himself. He's convinced that he approached the whole thing wrong, that it wasn't really his kind of law and he should've sent Mr. Santelli to an expert in criminal law. Liz, you should hear him talking. I've never heard Dad sound so down on himself, so defeated. It's really scary."

Elizabeth felt a knot forming in her stomach. "But—you told him that's crazy, didn't you? That he'd done everything he possibly could and it wasn't his fault?"

Steven sighed heavily. "I tried, but frankly it didn't do much good. Dad's pretty depressed about the whole field of law right now. He's had some more run-ins at the office with that young associate he told us about, and I think he's more convinced than ever that most of the lawyers around him are money-hungry, unethical creeps."

Elizabeth knew how hard her father had worked to prepare for this trial. The disappointment must be crushing. "What's going to happen to Mr. Santelli?" she asked.

"Dad doesn't know yet, but it doesn't look good. Lyle Jackson, Mr. Santelli's opponent for mayor, has been playing this to the hilt. There's no way Jackson would be as good a mayor as Mr. Santelli. The whole thing's so unfair."

"It's pretty rotten timing," she murmured. "Here Mom's just gotten the biggest break of her whole career, and Dad's feeling worse and worse about his!"

"Yeah, I know," Steven said. "And since everyone's read the paper today and knows about Mom's big coup, it's even worse. Somebody came up to Dad in the office today and congratulated him about Mom. He looked sad, Liz. He could really use a rest. It's a good thing our annual weekend at the lake is coming up."

Elizabeth didn't know what to say or do. She knew her father had tried his hardest, and as he himself—at least his old self—would have said—that was what mattered.

But she had a feeling that more was at stake this time. Mr. Wakefield's ego had taken a real battering in the courtroom, and it certainly wasn't going to help the situation at home.

"I guess Mom's going to be late," Elizabeth said awkwardly. It was seven-thirty, and there was still no sign of Mrs. Wakefield—no phone call, nothing. They had waited as long as they could to do something about dinner. "I could call her at the office—" Elizabeth began.

"No." Her father cut her off sharply. "Let's just fix something ourselves. Your mother obviously has work to do." There was a bitter edge to his voice.

"Let's just order in a pizza," Jessica said, reaching for the phone.

Mr. Wakefield paced back and forth. "Things are going to have to change around here. You've been eating entirely too much junk food," he grumbled.

"Daddy, we don't mind," Jessica said cheerfully.

"Well, *I* mind," he said shortly. Almost as if on cue, the back door opened, and Mrs. Wakefield rushed in, out of breath and looking at them with a mixture of affection and alarm.

"You haven't eaten yet, have you?" she cried, setting some bags down on the counter. "I wanted to surprise everyone and pick up some sandwiches at the deli, but it was closed. Then I went to three other places, and not a single one was still open. But I did manage to pick up some Chinese food."

"Great, Mom," Jessica said.

Elizabeth watched her mother and father closely. Neither one of them had looked at the other since Mrs. Wakefield walked in the door.

"I guess you had a busy day," Mr. Wakefield said at last.

"Oh, no," Mrs. Wakefield said with a false laugh. "Not at all! I was only late because we had a little meeting, nothing important . . ." She waved her hand dismissively, then took a deep breath. "Anyway, it looks like I made it. Let's set the table, girls." She gave them a forced smile. "I'm starved. I didn't have a single minute to grab a bite." She blushed. "I mean . . . well—"

"Never mind," Mr. Wakefield interrupted. "Let's just sit down and have some dinner. It's late already."

"Mom, can I watch this TV movie while I eat?" Jessica asked. "It's supposed to be great."

"Absolutely not," Mrs. Wakefield said. "We haven't even had a chance to talk to each other yet. And you know it's a rule in this household: no TV at mealtimes."

Mr. Wakefield eyed her stonily. "It seems to me," he muttered, "that a lot of rules around here are being broken these days. For instance, the rule about calling home if you think you're going to be late."

"You're right," Mrs. Wakefield said instantly. "I'm sorry. I got distracted and completely lost track of time." She began removing cardboard cartons from the paper bag.

"How was your day?" she asked Mr. Wakefield.

Dead silence greeted this question. "Ned?" she tried again.

"Everyone wanted to talk about the trial," Mr. Wakefield said.

"Oh, honey, what a shame, but I'm not surprised. You expected people to ask you about it, didn't you?"

"I may have expected it," Mr. Wakefield said defensively, "but I certainly hoped people would be tactful enough not to remind me of it every minute of the day!"

"Well, it's only human, Ned. People are going to be curious, and they're going to make comments."

Come on, Mom, Elizabeth thought, *can't you be a little more sympathetic?* Her mother's reasonable expression couldn't be very much consolation to her father at this point.

Luckily just then the phone rang. Steven answered it and passed the receiver to his father.

"Mmmm. Yes, I see. Yes, that makes sense," Mr. Wakefield said. "Well, Peter. I'm sorry to hear that, but I can see why you've reached that conclusion."

A minute later he hung up the phone. His face was pale, and he looked even more exhausted and depressed than when he had arrived home that afternoon.

"That was Peter Santelli. He's withdrawing from the mayoral race," he said slowly. "He feels that after all the bad press he's gotten, there isn't much point in continuing."

"Oh, no!" Mrs. Wakefield cried. "He shouldn't give up just like that! Peter has so many supporters in Sweet Valley. I'm sure he still stands a good chance of winning."

Mr. Wakefield gave her a look of cold anger. "Alice, trust me on this one. Peter knows what he's doing. He doesn't stand a chance, not with all the hype the trial has created. Instead of helping Peter, I made his situation worse," he added. "I'm a good part of the reason why Peter Santelli has to withdraw from the election."

Alice Wakefield looked as miserable as her husband. But it didn't seem as though there was any way the two of them could comfort each other.

Eight

"So, how does it feel now that your mother's a big hotshot designer?" Amy Sutton asked Jessica at lunchtime on Wednesday.

Jessica poked at her salad. "It's great," she said. "I keep waiting for my mom to tell me she's going to name a wing after me."

"Fat chance," Lila said, snitching one of Amy's french fries. "Hey, how's your father taking it? Isn't it hard on him now that he's just helped Mr. Santelli lose his chance of becoming mayor?"

"That isn't exactly how it happened, Lila. But I'm sure Daddy can cope. He's been a little blue, but he'll snap out of it."

"I wouldn't count on it," Amy said. "Don't you know how stressful competition can be to a marriage?"

Jessica shrugged. "Everyone makes such a big deal out of this stuff. My parents are fine." She grinned. "Besides, the more wrapped up they are in their own problems, the more freedom I have to worry about my *own* love life."

"You mean with the phantom phone caller?" Amy asked.

"What phantom phone caller?" Lila demanded.

This was just the minute Jessica had been waiting for. "Oh, nothing, Lila," she said dismissively. "It's just that I met this incredible guy through one of those party lines. You've heard about them, haven't you?" she added.

"Party line? What are you talking about?"

Jessica giggled. "You must be too busy with that video camera of yours, Lila. Why don't you try the phone sometime instead? It's not a bad way to fall in love, you know."

"Right," Amy intercepted, "if you're content to love a voice. But is this guy ever going to materialize in three-D?"

In fact, Jessica had been thinking about little else lately. She had to make Amy and Lila believe she was going to meet the guy of her dreams very soon.

"Well, Charlie's a little shy," she said. "That's why it's taking so long. But we're going to get together soon."

That evening Jessica was up in her room fuming. She had waited all this time before telling

Lila about the party line, and Lila had hardly even expressed any interest in it at lunch that day. It was clear to Jessica that she would actually have to have Charlie himself to dangle in front of Lila if she was going to prove anything. The previous night on the party line she had managed to extract Charlie's home phone number from him. Ever since lunch she'd been taking it out and looking at it. Now she made up her mind.

She punched in the number quickly, held her breath, and waited nervously. After a few rings, a low male voice answered.

"Is Charlie there?" she asked.

"This is Charlie," he said.

Jessica frowned. Not her Charlie, it wasn't. This voice sounded much older, much deeper. "Um—" she began uncertainly.

The man laughed. "I'll bet you want Charlie, Junior. Just a minute, please. I'll get him."

"That was my father," Charlie confirmed when he came onto the line a minute later. "Don't worry. It always confuses people."

Jessica was regaining her composure. "Hey, Charlie," she said, in what she thought was her sexiest voice, "do you realize this is the first time you and I have talked privately?"

"Yeah," he said softly. "I sure do, Jess. This is great. Why didn't we do this sooner? You know, talking to you is the brightest part of my day."

He's so romantic, Jessica thought.

"Do you have any idea how fabulous you are to talk to? You're so sweet, so funny, so interesting," he continued.

This was Jessica's favorite kind of conversation. She loved hearing a list of all her positive characteristics. In fact, she would have been happy to hear more, but it was time to get down to serious business.

"Well," she said teasingly, "if you think it's fun talking to me on the phone, wait till we get to talk in person."

"I can barely wait," Charlie whispered. "But you know, it's been so—so special talking this way. I'm not sure I'm ready to give up the surprise, are you?"

Jessica bit her lip. Was there some reason Charlie didn't want to meet her? She had to find out.

"What are you doing this weekend?" she asked bravely. "My friend Amy told me there's a great concert in Big Mesa—some new group from the East Coast—and I thought maybe you might want to go with me."

"Darn, I'd love to, Jess," Charlie said, sounding disappointed. "But my brother's coming home from Stanford for the weekend, and my

parents made me promise not to make plans."
He paused. "Do I get another chance?" he asked,
in a voice that made Jessica feel warm all the
way down to her toes.

"Sure," she said. "We'll get together some
other time, OK?"

"Definitely," Charlie said.

When Jessica hung up a few minutes later,
she felt totally confused. Was Amy right? Was
Charlie just a voice she'd never get to meet?

Elizabeth threw herself down on the couch in
the living room on Wednesday night and smiled.
Prince Albert was curled up in a corner, nap-
ping, Steven was reading a text for his legal
ethics course, Mrs. Wakefield was glancing
through some mail that had piled up, and Mr.
Wakefield was listening to music on his headphones and flipping through a magazine. The
mood was relaxed, and for once no one seemed
to be angry or tense.

"Ned!" Mrs. Wakefield exclaimed suddenly,
removing a letter from the stack of mail. "You
didn't tell me we'd been invited to your legal
fraternity's annual dinner!"

Mr. Wakefield took off his headphones. "What?"
he asked.

Mrs. Wakefield was reading the letter. "Psi

Epsilon is having their family dinner this Friday night. Why didn't you tell me about it? I love those things," she said, scanning the rest of the letter.

"To tell you the truth, I'm not sure I want to go," Mr. Wakefield said with a rueful laugh.

"Oh, come on, Ned," Mrs. Wakefield protested. "They're having wonderful speakers—a state supreme court justice, a leading criminal lawyer from San Francisco. Wouldn't it be wonderful for Steve and for the girls? You know we couldn't make it last year because we were out of town. And the girls have never been able to go before. Let's do it, Ned."

Mr. Wakefield frowned. "I don't know, Alice. You know I haven't been feeling so great about the legal world these days. I'm not sure I want to spend an evening surrounded by other lawyers who are just like the new associate in my office."

"Please, Ned!" Mrs. Wakefield was insistent. "I think it's exactly the sort of thing that could make you feel better about law! Don't you think so?" she asked, turning to Elizabeth and Steven.

"It could be interesting," Steven said neutrally.

"Uh, sure," Elizabeth said, even though she wasn't. "It sounds nice, if Dad wants to do it."

Mrs. Wakefield looked pleadingly at her husband.

"All right," Mr. Wakefield said reluctantly. "If the kids don't have plans and really want to go . . ."

"It's settled!" Mrs. Wakefield said triumphantly. "I'll RSVP right away." She paused, "You'll see, Ned. You'll be so glad we did it."

"Jessica!" Elizabeth pounded on her sister's door. "Come on, the rest of us are all ready to go. We can't keep waiting for you!"

Jessica sighed. "I've got to go, Charlie. I'm going to this legal fraternity dinner with my family. I'd much rather be meeting you somewhere," she added pointedly.

On Friday evening, despite all of her protests, Jessica was being dragged along to the Psi Epsilon party at Tosca's, a new Italian restaurant in Sweet Valley. There were about a zillion things she would rather be doing, starting with meeting Charlie somewhere and going all the way down the list to staying home and taking a bubble bath. But Mrs. Wakefield had been firm. This was supposed to be some kind of big treat for her father, and they were all going. No matter what.

"You're wearing that?" Elizabeth said incredulously when Jessica opened the door.

"Yeah. What's wrong with it? Lila loaned it

to me," Jessica said, twirling around so Elizabeth could get a better glimpse of her fuchsia mini dress and matching tights.

Elizabeth shook her head. "Well, I guess there'll be enough people around to cover you up," she said dryly. "Just try to stay out of the limelight, Jess. Tonight's supposed to cheer Daddy up, not make him ashamed of his family."

Jessica swept past her sister, her nose in the air. "Don't bug me, Liz. It's bad enough having to spend a boring evening listening to lawyers talking!"

"And don't bad-mouth lawyers," Elizabeth scolded. "Dad's really been depressed lately, Jessica. He needs his confidence boosted. What he doesn't need is for any of us to make him feel worse."

Jessica shrugged. She didn't feel like talking about it anymore. The truth was, she was still trying to figure out what was going wrong between her and Charlie. They had spoken twice in the last two days—once on the teen line, once alone. He still hadn't come up with a time that he could meet her.

When they were all ready, they piled into two cars. Jessica rode with her mother, and Elizabeth and Steven drove with Mr. Wakefield.

"Mom!" Jessica cried as soon as she got into

her mother's car. "You got a car phone! This is great!"

"Don't play with that, Jessica. I only use it in real emergencies," her mother warned. "It costs a fortune."

Jessica replaced the phone. She wondered if it cost more or less than what it cost to use the party line.

"I hope this dinner cheers your father up," her mother said, glancing in her rearview mirror. "He really seems blue today, don't you think?"

Jessica fiddled with her seat belt. "Yeah," she said. It made her feel uncomfortable talking about her father with her mother like this. Maybe Elizabeth was right, she thought suddenly. Maybe things really *had* been more tense around the Wakefield household than she'd been willing to admit.

But there wasn't time to worry about it now. Before she knew it, they were at the restaurant where they waited for the others and then stepped inside.

"Wow," Jessica said, grabbing Elizabeth's arm. "Look at all the cute men!"

The restaurant was packed. Everyone was milling around, sipping drinks, calling out greetings, and making small talk. Before they had taken four steps into the restaurant, the Wake-fields were engulfed.

"Ned!" A small, beaming man came up. "Sy Underwood, remember? We met at the last bash like this." He pumped Mr. Wakefield's hand. "And you must be Alice," he added, turning to Mrs. Wakefield. "You're quite a celebrity these days. I understand your firm is in charge of designing the new wing of the mall."

Mrs. Wakefield reddened slightly, "Yes," she said, slipping her arm through her husband's. "And what kind of law do you practice, Mr. Underwood?" she asked politely, trying to steer the conversation back on track.

"I'd much rather talk about design than law," he replied. "You know, I had a secret yen to be an architect when I was an undergraduate. In fact . . ."

Steven and Elizabeth looked at each other. The next ten people they ran into all made a big fuss over Mrs. Wakefield, too. Things were definitely going from bad to worse.

"Daddy looks like he's going to lose it," Jessica whispered to her sister.

"I know, Jess! What are we going to do? This is awful! Everyone's going on and on about Mom and not saying one single supportive thing to Daddy about his trial."

Jessica was about to respond when she was

cut off by Griffin Pierce, the young associate her father had been complaining about for the past couple of weeks. "Hello, Ned! I didn't know you were a member of Psi Epsilon!" he boomed, coming over to shake Mr. Wakefield's hand.

Griffin Pierce looked about thirty years old, going on fifty. Everything he wore was gray: gray suit, gray vest, gray tie. Mr. Wakefield introduced him to the rest of the family. "This is Griffin Pierce," he said. "You remember, our newest associate at the firm." He gave Griffin a pinched smile.

"I'm surprised you felt like showing up here tonight, Ned, after that disappointing decision from the judge to let Mr. Santelli's case go," Griffin said.

This remark brought a shocked silence from the Wakefield family. Elizabeth couldn't believe anyone could be so insensitive. Mr. Wakefield turned pale, then bright red. "Excuse me," he said and walked off, head held high. In fact, he walked straight out of the restaurant and into the parking lot, with the rest of the family chasing after him.

"Ned!" Mrs. Wakefield cried. "You're not going to let a silly comment like that bother you, are you?"

Mr. Wakefield spun on his heel, his eyes

blazing. "Don't speak to me like that. I don't need condescension from you," he said, furious.

Jessica felt her blood turn cold. She had never heard her father speak to her mother in that tone of voice. This time when Elizabeth grabbed her arm, she grabbed back.

"What do you mean?" Mrs. Wakefield faltered. "Wh-what kind of voice?"

"You know what I mean. You convinced me to come here tonight, Alice, and now I look like a fool. Well, I'm not going to put up with it. I didn't want to come in the first place and I'm not staying now!"

Mrs. Wakefield stared after him, her lower lip quivering. Before she could say another word, he had stormed across the parking lot to his car, leaving the rest of them watching with shock and horror as he sped away.

Nine

"You wouldn't believe how awful it was, Todd," Elizabeth said the next morning. She and Todd had just gone for a morning swim in the Wakefields' pool and were now eating breakfast. "I don't think I've ever seen my parents this mad at each other."

"What happened after he left? Did you guys follow him?"

"Mom was really angry. She felt like we'd made this big effort for Dad's sake and he was just being stubborn. She made us all go back in and pretend to enjoy ourselves. We only stayed for another half hour, but it seemed to drag on forever. I can't remember a more horrible night. All I could think about was Daddy, back at home by himself."

"Did they make up?" Todd demanded.

"I don't know," Elizabeth said as she poured some milk into her coffee. "They're not overtly fighting anymore. When I got up this morning, they were having breakfast together and they were behaving very politely." She shivered. "Like strangers."

Todd put a comforting hand on her arm. "They're obviously going through a rocky period, Liz. I'm sorry. It sounds awful for all of you."

Elizabeth shook her head helplessly. "It is. It's like sitting in a movie theater and watching a really suspenseful movie. You want to warn the hero and heroine to be careful because you can see the danger coming. But of course there's nothing you can do. I want to help them, but I don't know what to do."

Todd moved closer to her and gave her a hug. "Just act like you always do, only be a little more patient, a little more forgiving. Just wait it out with them. I know it will get better, Liz."

Elizabeth's eyes stung and she knew she was very close to tears. It was hard to put into words how terrifying it had been for her the night before, seeing her father's outburst and the effect it had on her mother. Her parents seemed to be moving further and further apart.

Not even Todd could totally understand. For the first time, Elizabeth realized how private her pain was. That was the thing about a family. You shared the good times with them, but when bad times came, you had to share those, too.

Mr. Wakefield was in his study when the doorbell rang.

"Alice," he called, "could you get that?"

"Sorry, dear. I'm on the phone with Sal, going over some designs. Could you get it?" Mrs. Wakefield called back.

Mr. Wakefield set his jaw and put down the memos he had been reading. Then he got up and went to open the front door.

Henry Patman and a man Mr. Wakefield didn't know were standing on the doorstep. Both men were wearing suits and ties.

"Hello, Henry," Mr. Wakefield said, surprised. "What brings you to this part of town?"

Mr. Patman was one of the richest men in Southern California. He was proud of everything he had accomplished and liked to let people know it. In fact, Henry Patman had his finger in everything in town—every deal, every transaction. He was a big businessman, a big socialite, a big wheeler and dealer.

"We were just having brunch nearby," Mr. Patman said, smoothing his tie, "and wondered if we might come in and have a word with you. About business," he added vaguely.

"You're welcome to come in," Mr. Wakefield said, looking quizzically past Mr. Patman to his companion.

"This is James Knapp," Mr. Patman continued. "I'm sure you've heard his name. James is a political analyst who was assisting in running Peter Santelli's campaign."

"Oh, yes," Mr. Wakefield said. "Well, please come in, both of you. Let's go into my study, where we can have some privacy."

Mr. Patman and Mr. Knapp followed Ned Wakefield into his study. Mr. Patman's eyes flicked over the array of diplomas and awards hanging on the walls. "Very distinguished career," he murmured. "Don't you think so, James?" he added.

Mr. Knapp nodded. "Mr. Wakefield, before I say another word, may I just tell you how courageous I think you've been, taking on the defense of Peter Santelli and fighting to uphold his name?"

Mr. Wakefield smiled, slightly embarrassed. "I don't know how courageous it was. That's what lawyers are supposed to do—defend people they believe are innocent."

"You see?" Mr. Patman said, almost jubilantly. "You see how much charisma he has? How much conviction?"

"You were right, Henry. Absolutely right."

Mr. Wakefield stared at the two men. "What's going on here?" he demanded.

"Listen, Ned," Mr. Patman said, settling back in a chair and crossing his legs, "A number of us had our hearts set on Peter's winning the election. You can't imagine how disappointed we are that he's been forced to pull out."

"Well, I know how terrible *I* feel about it," Mr. Wakefield said slowly.

"We've been thinking, and we were talking it over at lunch today. And James and I feel it would be wonderful to see you run for mayor, Ned," Mr. Patman said.

"What? Me?" Mr. Wakefield asked, obviously stunned.

Mr. Knapp got up and paced around the room. "You're a perfect candidate, Ned. You're young, strong, smart—with a wonderful background in law. You've got a beautiful family. You're honest. You're ethical. You're exactly what this community needs, and who this community will vote for," he added.

Mr. Wakefield shook his head. "I—listen, I'm flattered," he said slowly. "Extremely flattered. But I'm not sure—"

"It isn't as if we haven't given this matter a great deal of thought," Mr. Patman continued. "You may not have known this, Ned, but James

99

and I were backing Mr. Santelli's campaign."
He cleared his throat. "The fact is, we'd like to
see somebody good run against Jackson. We
don't think he'll do this town as much good as
somebody—well, somebody like you."

Mr. Wakefield got to his feet. "Are you asking *me* to run for mayor? But the election is only
a few months away!"

"We're aware of that, Ned, and we'd have to
work hard certainly. We'd have to get a lot of
good people together to help us. But we could
do it," Mr. Knapp said enthusiastically.

Mr. Wakefield walked slowly around his desk,
stopping for a second to pick up a paperweight
and roll it in his hand. On his desk was a
framed photograph of the whole family. His
eyes fell on it, then away. "In the first place, a
decision like this would take a great deal of
thought," he said slowly. "Even if I did want to
consider your offer, which I think is very gener-
ous, I'd have to see how my family would feel
about it."

"Yes," Mr. Knapp said soberly. "You would.
After all, running for office isn't something you
do lightly. We'd have to ask an enormous
amount from you. Your family would be making sacrifices as well. More publicity, less time
together. . . . Something like this can really take
its toll."

"As I said, this is quite a shock to me," Mr. Wakefield said, "I'm going to need some time to think it over, and above all, time to talk to my wife and children about it."

"That is fine, Ned," Mr. Patman said. "Just remember how much good you could do for the community! You'd make a wonderful mayor. I'm sure of it."

Mr. Wakefield smiled. "At the very least, let me just tell you both how flattered I am. I promise to give the idea a great deal of thought."

Jessica hadn't intended to listen in on her father's conversation. She had left the novel she had to read for English on the couch in his study. She was just going to knock on the study door when she heard a familiar voice. It took a minute for her to figure out that it was Mr. Patman. What could he be doing here? she wondered.

It would have been completely unthinkable not to lean in a little closer to try to get the gist of the conversation. That was when Jessica heard Mr. Patman urging her father to run for mayor.

Mayor!

Jessica spun around and flew upstairs. Elizabeth was in the bathroom, drying her hair, when Jessica burst in. "You're never going to believe what I just heard!" she gasped. "Daddy is going to run for mayor in Mr. Santelli's place!"

"What?" Elizabeth gasped, turning off the dryer and setting it on the counter.

"It's true, I swear. Mr. Patman is downstairs in Dad's study, and they're talking the whole thing over."

"Dad? Running for mayor?"

Jessica did a little dance of excitement. "Can you imagine how great it's going to be? We'll be famous. We'll probably meet all sorts of celebrities. Maybe Dad will be president one day," she added hopefully.

"I'm sure Daddy hasn't even made up his mind yet, Jess," Elizabeth said. "Maybe you heard wrong."

Jessica gave a cry of outrage, but Elizabeth put her hand up to quiet her. "Whether you heard wrong or not, don't you dare breathe one single word to anyone else. If Dad is seriously considering running for mayor, he's going to want to talk it over with Mom and us himself. So don't go making any announcements about Dad's new life as a mayor."

"All right, already," Jessica said. "What do you think I am, stupid?"

"Don't set yourself up," Elizabeth said with a laugh.

"Girls!" Mr. Wakefield called from downstairs.

"Have you seen your mother? I need to talk to her."

"See!" Jessica said.

"Oh, Jess, that doesn't mean a thing and you know it," Elizabeth said. "Let's go help Dad find Mom anyway," she added with a grin. "Just in case."

Mrs. Wakefield wasn't in the house. Jessica finally found her outside, just pulling out of the driveway.

She rolled down the car window. "Sorry," she said sheepishly. "I just thought I'd run over to the office with some of these specs. I wanted the others to look over them."

"Weren't you even going to let us know you were leaving?" Mr. Wakefield asked coldly.

"I thought I'd just be an hour or so. And you were all so busy, so—"

Mr. Wakefield folded his arms. "So it looks like you're going to spend most of another weekend working. Is that right?"

"Ned, I can't help it," Mrs. Wakefield said, nervously grasping the steering wheel. "I wish I didn't have to, but the designs are complex, and it's taking a lot longer than I thought it would!"

"I hope you're not planning on putting us through this next weekend," Mr. Wakefield continued. When she didn't respond, he added,

"You *do* remember what we're doing next weekend, don't you? We've got reservations at Lake Tahoe."

"Of course I remember!" Mrs. Wakefield snapped. The weekend at the rustic retreat had been an annual holiday for the past few years. "And don't worry. I won't ruin it for you. It just so happens that next weekend is one of the reasons I have to work so hard now. How else would I be able to get away for a weekend in the middle of this project?"

"Good question, Alice," Mr. Wakefield said sarcastically.

Elizabeth felt her heart sink as her mother backed her car into the street. She couldn't bear it when her parents snapped at each other like this. Last night her father had stormed off. Now it was her mother's turn. Were things ever going to improve between them?

Ten

Elizabeth always looked forward to the family's weekend at Lake Tahoe. They went to the same place every year, a wonderful rustic inn at the edge of the bluest, clearest mountain lake imaginable, with dozens of charming little cabins scattered around it. The Wakefields usually stayed in one of the cabins and cooked most of their meals on a barbecue. That was the plan for this trip as well.

"I wish we could stay in the main inn this year," Jessica confided to Elizabeth after school on Monday. "There aren't any phones in those cabins. That means I can't talk to Charlie for a whole weekend."

Elizabeth rolled her eyes. "Please," she said. "Since when are you so hooked on a guy that you can't tear yourself away for three days?" She looked suspiciously at her sister. "Besides, you haven't even met him yet, have you?"

"That's beside the point," Jessica snapped. She was extra sensitive about the subject because she just couldn't figure out why Charlie didn't seem that anxious to meet her. If she couldn't get him to agree to it soon, she was going to have to go back to square one with her "Top Lila" plan. And not only that, she would have to start looking elsewhere for a new boyfriend, too.

"You know, Charlie," Jessica began on Monday night, "my family's going to the mountains this weekend. Wouldn't it be great if we could get together before I went away?" She tried to make her voice sound casual, not demanding.

"Aww, Jess, you're going away this weekend? You're kidding! I was about to suggest that we meet in Sweet Valley on Saturday afternoon, spend the afternoon at the beach, hang out together, have dinner. I can't believe what rotten luck we have," he concluded.

"You really wanted to get together this weekend?" Jessica asked. She couldn't believe it. Bad luck was an understatement. This was completely and totally devastating. "Well," she went on, "how about Thursday? Or even Wednesday?"

"My car's in the shop," Charlie said sadly. "And it won't be out till Saturday morning."

"I could come over to *your* house," Jessica said brightly.

"Jessica," Charlie remonstrated gently, "I want our first meeting to be perfect. I don't want to meet over here with my parents around! Wouldn't it be better to wait till we can get the setting to be everything we want it to be?"

Jessica frowned. Waiting was not one of her favorite activities. "Maybe I can get out of going with my family this weekend. Then we could spend Saturday together," she said.

"You wouldn't want to do that. Your family would never like me then. And believe me, Jess, I want your family to like me."

When Jessica hung up the phone, she couldn't shake the feeling that something was seriously wrong. If Charlie liked her as much as he claimed he did, why wasn't he as impatient to get together as she was? Did he think she might be disappointing in person?

Jessica sat for a long time on her bed, staring sadly out her window. She couldn't remember the last time she had been so excited about meeting a boy. She thought about Charlie all the time. She went over and over their conversations, trying to remember every little thing he said. Each evening she looked forward to hearing his voice on the phone again. She was dying to meet him. She just didn't feel she could wait any longer.

And she didn't like the feeling that he *could* wait. She was just going to have to speed up their meeting—and make sure that once he'd seen her, he would never be content to settle for the telephone again!

Mrs. Wakefield didn't make it home for dinner on Monday night or Tuesday night that week. She was working constantly, getting to the office first thing in the morning and staying till late at night. Now that Steven had gone back to college, Elizabeth thought the house felt even emptier and less organized than it had before.

"Poor Prince Albert," she said, scratching the dog behind his ears. "No one's been paying much attention to you around here, have they?" Maybe this weekend would pull them together again. Her parents could definitely use a rest.

But from the way her mother had been talking, the long-planned-for weekend was just one more obligation. "I don't see how I'm going to manage to juggle everything," her mother had said the night before. 'Everyone else in the group is planning to work this weekend. I wonder . . ."

Mr. Wakefield had merely raised his eyebrows at her and said nothing. But this time Elizabeth felt that she couldn't contain herself. "Mom, you can't back out of the trip. You need a vacation—we all do!" she exclaimed.

"Oh, sweetheart, I know," her mother said sadly. "But I'm really buried in this stuff. I'm not sure it's a good idea for me to go away for the whole weekend. Maybe if I came up a day later than the rest of you . . ."

"Alice," Mr. Wakefield said, "there are other things in life besides work."

Mrs. Wakefield bit her lip. "I'm sure I can get through most of this by Friday, anyway," she said.

"And another thing," Mr. Wakefield said. "We're going to have an understanding before we even set foot out the door on Friday. No work up in the mountains. The point of this weekend is to spend time together as a family, right?"

"Um, right," Mrs. Wakefield said weakly. She looked at her husband for a long moment. "Ned, wasn't there something you said you wanted to talk to me about tonight?"

"Not now, Alice. It'll have to wait," Mr. Wakefield said in a bitter voice. Before she could say another word, he picked up the paper he'd been working on and left the room.

*   *   *

Todd came home with Elizabeth on Wednesday after school. They both had homework to do, and these days the Wakefields' house was the quietest place to work during the week. "Let's go outside and work on the patio," Elizabeth suggested, handing Todd a cold can of soda.

She was stopped on her way outside by the telephone ringing. It was Julia, her mother's assistant. "Your mother is at the mall this afternoon, going over drafts with some of their execs," Julia told Elizabeth. "She asked me to send messages home. Could you tell her that she needs to call Sal as soon as she possibly can tonight? Sal says it's urgent."

"Sure, Julia," Elizabeth said, writing down the message. "Boy, my mother hasn't had a minute for herself, has she?" she added. *Or for any of us*, she added silently. *Especially for Dad.*

"Oh, well, this project is wearing us all down. But your mother is a strong woman. She'll be fine," Julia said.

Elizabeth bit her lip. She didn't particularly like the way that sounded. If she could get Julia to be just a little bit more concerned about her mother, maybe she'd help pressure Mrs. Wakefield to take the weekend off.

"I'm just hoping our weekend up in the mountains will help. She needs a break," Elizabeth said.

"Oh?" Julia said.

"You know how it is," Elizabeth added quickly. "When you start to get run down, you just can't perform as well. I wouldn't want that to happen to my mother," she added.

"Neither would I," Julia said, sounding concerned. "But I hadn't realized she was planning to go away for sure this weekend. I thought—"

Elizabeth had to think fast. If her mother was already beginning to back out of the weekend, she needed some extra pressure—from Julia and the others in the office—to make sure she went to Tahoe after all.

"Listen, Julia," she interrupted. "You're going to have to help me on this one," Elizabeth said quickly. "Can't you guys gang up on my mom and insist that she go away? She really is under a lot of stress, and I'm not kidding when I say she needs a break."

"Well," Julia said, somewhat reluctantly, "we could try, I guess. But you know your mother," she added. "She's far too involved in this project right now to tear herself away, especially to go up to an isolated cabin at Lake Tahoe, where none of us can even get hold of her."

"There's a phone at the main inn," Elizabeth said slowly. "It's just—well, we don't usually

111

give it out. We try to make the whole weekend a time just for us."

"I have an idea," Julia said. "Why don't you give me the name of the place where you'll be staying and the phone number where we can reach you—just in case some sort of emergency comes up? If I know I can reach your mother, I'll feel better about convincing her to go."

Elizabeth wasn't sure how great an idea it was to give Julia the name of the inn, or its number. It had been a long-standing rule in the Wakefield household that family vacations were strictly workfree. What if there was an emergency and Julia *did* call? Her father would be furious.

But on the other hand, Julia could be trusted to discriminate truly urgent calls from less important interruptions. She had to do it, Elizabeth thought. This was the only way that she could think of to get her mother's whole office to rally behind her and insist she take off for the weekend.

"Hang on, Julia. Let me get the number from my father's desk," she said. "Try your hardest to get her to go," she begged. She felt a little bit guilty about the conversation. After all, she had practically twisted Julia's arm to get her to agree to this. But if it worked, it would be worth it.

"You can count on me," Julia said cheerfully

after Elizabeth gave her the number. "Don't worry, Liz. Your mother will get the break she needs. I promise."

Elizabeth closed her eyes. A perfect daydream image came to her: the whole family sitting together on the dock, laughing, telling stories, diving into the clear blue water . . .

It was going to be a wonderful weekend. And Elizabeth was going to make sure that her mother was there to enjoy it.

Eleven

"I can't believe we're actually going—all of us—without a hitch," Elizabeth whispered to her sister Friday afternoon. Mr. and Mrs. Wakefield were outside, packing a few last things into the car before setting off for Tahoe. Steven had just arrived, and now they were ready to set off for the mountains.

"I know," Jessica whispered back. "And Mom even managed to get off work this afternoon. It's a miracle."

Elizabeth nodded. For the past few days things had been quiet around the house, but she had been unduly anxious about the trip. Would her mother be able to come, after all? Would they manage to have a good time?

By seven-thirty Friday evening, all her worries seemed to have been in vain. The Wakefields had checked in at the main inn, picked up the key to their charming redwood cabin, and unpacked their clothes. The cabin was perfect: three cozy bedrooms, a small kitchen, and a tiny living room with a fireplace. Even Jessica seemed to get over her melancholy about the missed opportunity to spend time with Charlie this weekend. "This is great!" she exclaimed. "It's even nicer than last year."

"It's so peaceful!" Mrs. Wakefield said, twirling around with a smile. "No phones, no disturbances . . . it's blissful."

"Smell the pine needles!" Mr. Wakefield said appreciatively.

The sun was just setting out on the lake, and everyone agreed there was enough time for a refreshing dip in the lake before cooking out on the grill. Elizabeth felt the tension ease out of her as she changed quickly into her suit and raced out after the others, the soft pine needles like a carpet under her bare feet. *I was nuts to be so worried*, she told herself. *It's just like Todd and everyone else has been saying. Mom and Dad have had some rough moments, but that doesn't mean their marriage is in trouble. From now on, everything is going to be just fine.*

"Last one out to the float has to cook dinner!" Jessica cried, hurling herself off the dock and splashing water onto her mother.

"Jess, watch it," Mrs. Wakefield scolded playfully. Elizabeth, who didn't feel like racing, swam

116

around under the dock. She could hear her parents' voices floating above her.

"I'm so glad we've finally got some time together," she heard her mother say.

"Me, too," her father responded. "Alice, listen, there's something important I'd like to talk to you about later on."

"Whoops," Mrs. Wakefield said. "Steve's calling me from out on the float. I think I'll take a dip now."

Then Elizabeth heard a splash as her mother dived into the water.

For the next half hour or so, the Wakefields luxuriated in the last light of the day, enjoying the warm lake, the beautiful sunset, and the smell of the pine forest behind the cabin. When Mr. Wakefield suggested that they dry off and start dinner, none of them wanted to come out of the water. Even so, the good mood seemed to last as preparations for cooking began. Everyone was so cheerful, so relaxed. Elizabeth felt the tension creep out of her bit by bit.

"This place is beautiful, isn't it?" Jessica said, slipping into her sweatshirt. "Daddy, don't you think Sweet Valley needs a beautiful inn and cabins like this? Maybe when you run for mayor—"

Elizabeth poked her hard in the ribs, and

Jessica clapped her hand over her mouth. "Whoops," she said.

"How on earth—" Mr. Wakefield began incredulously.

But Mrs. Wakefield's voice was the one that could be heard loudest above the confusion. "Run for mayor? What are you talking about, Jessica?"

"I haven't the faintest idea where you heard that, Jessica, but I haven't made any decisions yet about whether or not to run. Nor do I intend to, until I've had time to discuss it with your mother—and with the rest of you."

"I can't believe this!" Mrs. Wakefield cried. "Do you mean to say that you are seriously considering running for mayor—and that I don't even know about it? Did you plan on mentioning it to me, or were you just going to save it as a surprise?" Hurt and bitterness filled her voice.

"Alice, I tried to find time to talk to you, but you've been so busy," Mr. Wakefield protested.

But there was no quieting Mrs. Wakefield's anger. "That's preposterous. I know I've been busy, but you could have told me how important it was that we talk. You could have said *something*." Her face had turned very pale. "I think it's a ludicrous idea. You don't have any political experience. Who even suggested that you think about it?"

Now Mr. Wakefield was starting to get angry. "For your information, Alice, years of juridical experience count for something. I am a lawyer, remember? And I've served on a number of civic committees. I don't think it's 'ludicrous' at all."

"I'm sorry," Mrs. Wakefield amended. "I didn't mean that. It's just—well, I suppose I'm surprised, that's all. It's an idea that's going to take some getting used to."

"Well, I felt the same way when Mr. Patman and his friend James Knapp came over and suggested it to me. But the more thought I've given it over the past week, the less crazy it seems to me."

Mrs. Wakefield glanced quickly at Steven, Jessica, and Elizabeth. "Let's talk about it more later," she said.

Elizabeth let out a deep breath. She hadn't even realized until that moment she'd been holding her breath since her mother's explosive outburst. Were things going to settle down again, or had the entire weekend been ruined by Jessica's little slip?

"I can't believe you did that," Elizabeth snapped, glaring at her sister. "Didn't you even stop to think? You promised me you weren't going to blab what you heard about Dad."

"Quit yelling at me. I couldn't help it," Jessica said, hunching her shoulders defensively. "Besides, I think it's good that it's finally out in the open."

The girls were in their room in the cabin, changing into nightgowns. Outside Elizabeth could hear crickets chirping and branches rustling gently. But the mood in the cabin didn't feel peaceful and serene to her anymore. She felt as nervous as she had before they came to the lake.

"Out in the open," she repeated incredulously. "Jess, don't you ever feel sorry about anything you do? Can't you admit that what you did was wrong?"

"Liz, cut it out," Jessica said angrily, covering up her ears. "I'm not going to listen this stuff. Besides, all you've done for the last couple of weeks is worry about Mom and Dad. We can't be responsible every time they have an argument. If they're not getting along with each other, that isn't my fault!" Her eyes flashed defiantly.

Elizabeth didn't answer. An enormous feeling of sadness welled up in her. For as long as she could remember, she had heard friends' stories about their parents' troubles with a mixture of sympathy and incomprehension. Her own parents had almost never had a fight, as far as she could tell. The Wakefields' courtship and marriage was like something out of a fairy tale. They met, they fell in love, they got married, and they really did live happily ever after.

Until now.

Her sister was right about one thing. It wasn't up to the twins or Steven to try to smooth relations between their parents. They were going to have to resolve whatever was wrong between them all on their own.

It made Elizabeth even sadder to have quarreled with Jessica. It felt more acutely than ever as if their family was coming apart at the seams. This weekend at Tahoe had always been such a wonderful time of togetherness. Now they seemed like five separate people going in five different directions.

Elizabeth didn't have the faintest idea of what it would take to make them feel like a family again.

"OK," Mr. Wakefield said a little while later, after everyone had changed into their nightclothes and bathrobes. "Time for charades!"

This was one of the most sacred traditions of their weekend at the lake. Once everyone was ready for bed, they made hot chocolate and played charades. The sillier the game was the better.

"I'm ready," Steven called, coming out into the living room in his tartan bathrobe. The twins were already curled up on the sofa, looking at the last glowing embers of the fire.

"Where's your mother?" Mr. Wakefield asked Steven.

"I'm not sure. I thought she was out here," Steven said.

Mr. Wakefield frowned, then crossed the living room and tapped gently on the door to the third bedroom. "Alice?"

"Come on in," she called in a distracted voice.

Mr. Wakefield opened the door, and they could see Mrs. Wakefield sitting cross-legged on the bed, engrossed in a folder of papers.

"Hey," Mr. Wakefield said. "I thought we promised—no work." He said it teasingly, but he didn't sound happy. "Come on out here and play charades. We're on vacation. Remember?"

Mrs. Wakefield brushed her hair back with one hand. "I'll be there in a minute," she murmured, straightening the papers and placing them neatly in the folder. She read one last document before shutting the folder.

"Fine," Mr. Wakefield declared. "Listen, guys, maybe charades isn't such a good idea this year.

We're all tired. Why don't we just call it a night?"

The twins and Steven looked at one another in surprise. None of them wanted to beg their father to play. It was one of those moments—and there had been a lot of them lately—when there was just no point in letting their disappointment show.

There's always tomorrow, Elizabeth thought sadly. *Just because the first day of the weekend didn't go perfectly doesn't mean tomorrow won't be better.*

Twelve

Elizabeth awoke to a sparkling, clear day the next morning. The fresh mountain air had just a slight bite to it. Jessica was already up, but she'd left her bed unmade and wads of her clothing balled up everywhere. Elizabeth rubbed her eyes sleepily.

"Wake up already!" Jessica said, bursting through the door. "Daddy wants to go canoeing on the lake."

Elizabeth groaned. "What are you doing up so early? Since when do you wake up before me?" She looked suspiciously at her sister.

"It's love," Jessica said dramatically. "It's turning me into an insomniac. Since I met Charlie, I haven't had a single night when I didn't dream about him."

"But you haven't met him yet, silly. Remember?"

"Very funny, Liz. You know what I mean,"

she said. "Besides, I'm going to meet him—this very week! I could've met him this weekend if we weren't here at the lake," she added.

Elizabeth shrugged. She didn't feel like arguing about her sister's phantom boyfriend right now. "All right, Jess. Just let me put on my suit and I'll be right there."

She dressed in a flash and ran down to the lake after her sister. Steven and Mr. Wakefield were already in a canoe, wearing life preservers. "You two get in that canoe," he said, pointing with his paddle.

"Where's Mom?" Elizabeth asked.

"Oh, she didn't feel like coming," Mr. Wakefield said calmly. "Don't worry," he added. "We can all do something together this afternoon."

It was beautiful out on the lake, but Elizabeth couldn't stop wishing her mother were there with them. What was the point of a family weekend if they didn't do things together? "Mom should've come. She would have really enjoyed this," she said once they had paddled to a secluded inlet.

"Sweetheart, it's OK if people don't always get to do the same things at the same time," her father said soothingly. "Anyway, your mother said she wanted to fix us a surprise lunch."

Elizabeth blushed and stared into the water,

feeling ashamed for overreacting again. She could feel Jessica looking at her disapprovingly.

She made up her mind to forget about the tensions of the night before, and once she did, the rest of the morning was wonderful. They floated slowly back to the dock in the canoes, stopping halfway for a leisurely dip in the lake. When they got back to the cabin, Mrs. Wakefield seemed to be in a wonderful mood. She had started the barbecue and was just waiting for them before she grilled the fish.

"I should've asked you to catch some," she said, her eyes twinkling. "I hope there's enough here for my hungry family."

"So do I," Mr. Wakefield agreed. "I don't know about the rest of you, but I'm starving."

The twins set the picnic table down by the water's edge, and soon the fish was grilled to perfection. Steven brought a salad out from the kitchen, and they all sat down to eat.

"Boy, this is the life," Mrs. Wakefield said, leaning back to feel the sun on her face.

"It's been a long time since we've had a day like this," Mr. Wakefield said quietly. "It's one of the reasons I'm reluctant to take Mr. Patman up on his offer to run for mayor. Appealing as it is in some ways, I know it would take me away from all of you. And I'm not sure I could tolerate that."

"I know what you mean," Mrs. Wakefield responded. "Starting a political campaign would be exciting, but it could be pretty intrusive, too."

Elizabeth swallowed hard. She saw her parents give each other a long, meaningful look, and she felt goosebumps rising on her arms. Were they finally beginning to realize how little they had been communicating with each other lately? Maybe this weekend really would bring them closer together.

Mr. Wakefield was about to speak when a boy on a bicycle came out of the woods, his face red and his chest heaving from exertion. "Mrs. Wakefield?" he asked. "I'm from the main inn— I'm the owner's son—and my dad asked me to tell you there's a telephone call for you. They say it's urgent."

"Urgent? Who could possibly be calling me here?"

Mr. Wakefield frowned in annoyance. "I thought we agreed we wouldn't tell a soul where we were going to be," he said.

"We did—and I didn't. Nobody knew."

"They said it had to do with some sort of design project," the boy continued.

Mr. Wakefield balled up his napkin and threw it down, enraged. "Great, Alice. Thanks a lot for honoring our promise. It's not bad enough that your job is ruining life at home. Now it has to ruin our life here, too!"

Mrs. Wakefield jumped to her feet, her eyes blazing and her face pale. "Go on ahead," she said to the boy. "Tell them I'll be there as fast as I can."

She didn't say a single word to Mr. Wakefield or anyone else. Elizabeth felt sick inside. It was all her fault. She was the one who had blabbed the phone number of the inn to Julia. But it was too late to do anything about it now.

"Mom—I have to tell you something," Elizabeth stammered. She followed her mother inside the cabin as soon as she got back from the inn.

"I gave Julia the phone number. I know I shouldn't have, but I was afraid you'd be too worried about leaving the office for a whole weekend unless she insisted you go. And she really couldn't promise to do that without knowing where you were going to be."

"Oh, sweetie, you poor thing," Mrs. Wakefield said, giving her a hug. "You look so worried!"

"Well, I am," Elizabeth admitted. "I know I'm the one to blame, and I didn't want Daddy blaming it on you."

Mrs. Wakefield turned away, a pained expression on her face. "Your father shouldn't have jumped to conclusions," she said shortly. "He should have known I wouldn't have broken my word. The truth is, your father has been looking for reasons to get angry with me all day."

Elizabeth didn't know what to say. Why was her mother confiding in her like this? "Why would he want to get angry?" Liz asked uncertainly.

"I'm not sure. I know he's resentful of the amount of time I've been putting into this project. It's turning into one of these situations where neither one of us can possibly win. I find myself trying to hide work, and he gets upset with me, so I'm even less open with him, and it just goes on and on."

"Oh, Mom," Elizabeth said, throwing her arms around her mother. "I'm so frightened. I don't want you and Daddy to be fighting."

Mrs. Wakefield stroked her hair. "Sweetheart, neither do I." She sighed sadly. "Neither do I."

Thirteen

Most of the magic had gone out of the weekend for Elizabeth by Saturday night. The strain between her parents was so evident that it was hard for any of them to ignore it. None of the customs from previous years felt natural or fun. They had gone for a hike that afternoon in almost total silence. There was none of the usual joking or kidding around. They ate dinner at the inn, and Elizabeth noticed her parents barely exchanged one word. They each talked to the twins and Steven, in strained, cheerful voices, but it was obvious they were avoiding each other.

When they got back from dinner, Mr. Wakefield made a fire, and they all sat down in the living room with the lights out.

"It's so clear out," Mrs. Wakefield said, peering out the window. "It'll probably be another gorgeous day tomorrow."

"Hey, can we go horseback riding? I saw a poster in the lodge for group rides," Jessica piped up.

Elizabeth's mood lifted. She had adored riding since she was a little girl. "That sounds great," she said.

"It sure does. I'd love to go for a ride," Mrs. Wakefield said enthusiastically.

"What about you, Dad?" Steven asked.

Mr. Wakefield sighed. He didn't look like he was feeling particularly enthusiastic about anything right then. "Well, if the rest of you want to go . . ." he said.

By the time the fire died out, they had decided. They would get up at the crack of dawn, have a hearty breakfast, and set out on horseback to explore. Elizabeth was looking forward to it, but she was so worried about her parents' behavior now that it was hard to focus on anything else.

"You'll feel better in the morning," Jessica murmured sleepily when Elizabeth tried to tell her how she was feeling after they got into bed.

And, in fact, Jessica turned out to be right. It was another bright, sparkling day, and they got up early enough to see the sunrise. When they were all dressed and ready, Elizabeth looked around at her family and smiled. At last they would be spending the whole day together, as a family.

They had arranged with the owners of the inn to pick up their horses at nine o'clock. Elizabeth's was a beautiful gray mare, Jessica's a palomino. Mrs. Wakefield had a dappled roan, and Steven and Mr. Wakefield had chestnut stallions. They had all mounted, and the horses were prancing around, eager to get started, when Mrs. Jenkins, the owner of the inn, came outside, waving to them.

"Mrs. Wakefield? There's a phone call for you. They say it's urgent."

"What's going on, Alice?" Mr. Wakefield said sharply.

"Ride on ahead. I'll meet you guys up at the big meadow in a few minutes," she said, not looking at her husband.

"Fine," Mr. Wakefield said in a bitter voice. And with a cluck to his horse, he led the way up through the woods to the meadow.

"Mom's taking forever!" Jessica wailed. The weather was already beginning to get warm, and the horses were impatient standing still.

Elizabeth shifted in her saddle, giving her twin a murderous look. Didn't Jessica know the first thing about tact? It was obvious their father was furious as it was. He didn't need reminding.

Just then Mrs. Wakefield galloped up, her blond hair shining in the sunlight, her face flushed from exertion. *Fall in love with her again, Daddy*, Elizabeth pleaded silently. *Don't be angry. Can't you see how beautiful she is?*

"Sorry," Mrs. Wakefield said. "It couldn't be helped. There was a disaster in the office last night. Sal had this brilliant idea to use interactive software to design part of the new wing. Well, the computer went down, and we lost almost everything."

Mr. Wakefield looked stiffly ahead. "So, can we go on now and enjoy the rest of our day?" he asked.

"Well, as a matter of fact, it looks like I'm going to have to head back home. They haven't been able to recover everything, and we're going to have to go over a lot of the designs we originally laid out, and with the deadline coming up—" She paused for a moment and looked at each one of them. "I feel awful about it, but I think I'd really better go." She took a deep breath. "It isn't like I'm leaving *that* much earlier than you are. I mean, you're going to leave around six this evening, and by the time you get back, I'll be done, and we can all have dinner together, and—"

"Alice," Mr. Wakefield interrupted. "That isn't the point. This weekend was set aside for us—all of us—as a family."

"I know that, Ned, but I can't. . . . Look, it's only a few hours difference," she tried again.

"Mom, you can't go back," Steven said anxiously. "We only came up in one car!"

"I checked with the innkeepers. There's a bus leaving in half an hour. If I just gather some of my stuff together right away, I can make it."

Mr. Wakefield's eyes filled with fury. "It's astonishing to me to see how little respect you have for this family right now, Alice. You've always been the one who's said that family commitments come first."

"They do come first! But I can't abandon the design team, either. They need me!" Mrs. Wakefield cried.

Elizabeth felt her eyes fill with tears. "We need you too, Mom," she choked out.

"Look, I've asked all of you before, and I'm going to ask you again. I have to work extra hard now that my firm has been chosen for this project. I need your support and patience right now. I don't like my being away from you anymore than you do. I have to go now. I'm going to ride back to the inn and let them take the horse for me. Mrs. Jenkins said she'd give me a ride to the cabin to get my things."

"I'm sorry I even bothered to worry about how running for mayor would affect the family," Mr. Wakefield said coldly. "Since you obviously couldn't care less, why should I? For your information, Alice, you're not going to be the only one with extraordinary commitments anymore. I'm going to tell Henry Patman that the answer is yes. I'll run for mayor. So what if I won't be home anymore? It obviously won't make any different at all to you!"

Elizabeth felt her breath catch in her throat. Each word her father said seemed to tear at her. She could see from the shocked expression on Jessica's and Steven's faces that they were feeling the same way she was, terrified—and numb.

"Do whatever you please," Mrs. Wakefield said. "I'll see you tonight at home."

"Alice, if you take off right now, you're doing more than just walking out on a weekend," Mr. Wakefield said. "You're walking out on me and the kids, too. Why don't you just stop and think for a second what that means."

"Are you threatening me, Ned?"

"All I'm saying is that I can't stand this anymore. If you leave now, you're leaving me. You're leaving our marriage."

Elizabeth thought she was going to faint. She heard a buzzing in her ears and could barely sit up on her horse. "Mom, don't!" she cried.

But it was too late. Mrs. Wakefield had already turned her horse around and was headed for the inn. Elizabeth couldn't hold back her tears. She didn't know who to look at or what to say.

She felt as though her life was ending. Where before there had been solid ground to stand on, now there was nothing. Was this really it, then? Did this mean that her parents were going to throw away more than twenty years of marriage?

What's going to happen to the Wakefield family? Find out in Sweet Valley High *#66,* **WHO'S TO BLAME.**

Coming next month: the second Sweet Valley High Super Star Edition, **BRUCE'S STORY.**

Arrogant, spoiled Bruce Patman is in for the fight of his life! Bruce's grandfather has set up a contest between Bruce and his cousin Roger—and the prize is control over the Patman millions!

Series
Don't miss any of the Caitlin trilogies
Created by Francine Pascal

There has never been a heroine quite like the raven-haired, unforgettable beauty, Caitlin. Dazzling, charming, rich, and very, very clever Caitlin Ryan seems to have everything. Everything, that is, but the promise of lasting love. The three trilogies follow Caitlin from her family life at Ryan Acres, to Highgate Academy, the exclusive boarding school in the posh horse country of Virginia, through college, and on to a glamorous career in journalism in New York City.

Don't miss Caitlin!